C000151769

About the Author

Peter Storm found his love of horror, growing up in Cornwall and Dartmoor, exploring the moors and finding eerie locations; watching Hammer House Horror, and reading Edgar Allen Poe, HG Lovecraft, along with Graham Masterton. He found the local ghost stories fascinating, wanting to explore more in search of haunted locations. He found that he could create and expand on the tales, creating his own style of horror. He now lives on the south coast, with his partner, where he continues to write and travel.

The Chine

Peter Storm

The Chine

Vanguard Press

VANGUARD PAPERBACK

© Copyright 2023
Peter Storm

The right of Peter Storm to be identified as author of
this work has been asserted by him in accordance with the
Copyright, Designs and Patents Act 1988.

All Rights Reserved

No reproduction, copy or transmission of this publication
may be made without written permission.
No paragraph of this publication may be reproduced,
copied or transmitted save with the written permission of the
publisher, or in accordance with the provisions
of the Copyright Act 1956 (as amended).

Any person who commits any unauthorised act in relation to
this publication may be liable to criminal
prosecution and civil claims for damages.

A CIP catalogue record for this title is
available from the British Library.

ISBN 978 1 80016 838 1

*Vanguard Press is an imprint of
Pegasus Elliot Mackenzie Publishers Ltd.*
www.pegasuspublishers.com

This is a work of fiction. Names, characters, businesses, places,
events and incidents are either the product of the author's imagination or
used in a fictitious manner. Any resemblance to actual persons, living or
dead, or actual events is purely coincidental

First Published in 2023

**Vanguard Press
Sheraton House Castle Park
Cambridge England**

Printed & Bound in Great Britain

Dedication

To Magda for believing in my writing.

Acknowledgements

To Rose Downs, Graham and Jo Verrall. For reading and liking the manuscript.

Studland bay, in the mid-19th century, as it is today, was always a tranquil haven; a much-loved region for the wealthy and privileged gentry. Victorians had been coming to the nearby hamlets of Bournemouth and Swanage for the past few years. They believed that the vast expanse of scented pines, mixed with the sea air, supplied a vital road to recovery for the sick and ageing. People were desperate to escape the grime and stench of London's streets, with its smoke and smog-laden air. Natural beauty was abounded in every direction along the bay, edged by the spacious, ever-stretching golden sands of its beaches. Nearby woodland walks offered a variety of pine-scented trails. Romantic walks that filtered away through the tall, aged pines were a fresh escape for the wealthy. Not surprising, then, that landowners had built vast mansions along the coastal area.

One such noble was Sir Nathaniel Ballard. Gifted with a region of the heathland from the crown, Ballard had been a wealthy sea merchant who had vast dealings in the trade routes of the West Indies. This had made Nathanial Ballard a favourite in the aristocracy circles. His tales entertained the royal court, and his wealth made him powerful new friends. He soon became a popular man, with influential people. He built his own estate, a beautiful mansion house set in the middle of the heath, surrounded by a picturesque, landscaped garden, with romantic walks through the woods to the nearby beaches.

On this dark, late autumn evening, there was nothing romantic or picturesque about his estate. Under the cover of night, this unlit region was hiding a true evil, one that was about to strip Nathaniel Ballard from all he had strived to get. He was soon to be cast aside from his family, destined to walk down a dark road of no return. Once a respected merchant, soon to be a deranged madman — a shadow of his former self — Nathanial Ballard was unaware of what was to become of him. Blinded by rage and heartbreak, caused by the loss of his one true love, Anabelle, who, like hundreds before her, died from consumption. Nathanial was blind to the disease, claiming so many lives in the era. His heartbreak became a rage that was driving him insane.

On this night, just one solemn light shone from what was once his beloved manor house. A lamp placed at the kitchen window, standing out like a beacon at the far end of the gardens, ready to guide someone home through the darkness. The sound of a light tapping drifted across the garden as it penetrated the silence. On this late August night, the heat of the summer still hung in the air. A warm, night breeze carried the sound into the pines, where it echoed through the trees, fading away to the beach. Once more, the slight tapping broke the silence before it echoed away into the darkness. It was emanating from a small bunker on the side of the garden. Inside, Nathaniel Ballard and his trusted friend, Leandro, were finishing bricking up a wall they had been working on for the past few days. The wall had halved the room, and their work was just about finished. All that he needed was the final few bricks, and the opposite side of the room would be closed off.

Not speaking, they set about the task at hand, Nathaniel tapping his friend on the shoulder, pausing the work, every few minutes. Shielding the small lamp, he would peer up the stone stairs, checking they were alone, before passing his companion another brick, urging him to continue. Leandro kept looking across to his friend, who held up the lamp, shedding light on the proceedings. Leandro was not sure they were doing the right thing. Yet Nathaniel's face held a fierce stern look, no sign of remorse or regret showing. Leandro knew better than to challenge Nathaniel. Hence, he kept going, laying brick after brick in silence, hoping that his friend might ask him to stop, admitting it was wrong.

Even as the last brick was laid, they heard nothing from the other side. Leandro leant forward, peering into the darkness on the other side of the room. He saw nothing. The lamp behind him offered a small amount of light. He backed away from the space, letting what light there was to pass by into the blackness. Still, he could detect nothing. The blackness of their actions seemed to have added to the already dark room.

Suddenly, from within the blackness, a face appeared, peering back through the hole. It was a boy's

13

face. Leandro jumped back, startled by the appearance. He crashed to the floor, his gaze fixed on the hole. Large, white, clear eyes stared down at him, the pupils flicking from side to side, as the eyes began scanning the other side of the room. They held Nathaniel's gaze for a second, then from behind the wall a muffled voice whispered. Leandro rose to his feet, backing away from the wall, peering over his shoulder at his comrade.

"What is he saying? Some odd accent, African, Haitian, I don't know," Leandro said.

"Who cares? Just get on with it. The black devil can say whatever he wants."

"What if they are casting voodoo spells at us? Listen, they are all whispering now," he gasped.

Leandro was now backing into his friend. He looked scared, concerned that they had gone too far this time.

"Behind that barrier, they can perish. They can cast dammed spells all night if they want to. Brick it up, man, then prop that cross against the wall. They can try to get past our god. Bloody voodoo or not, we should never have brought them here."

"I am positive this was all a mishap. It was nothing to do with these youngsters."

"God dammit, man, get on with it. Do not start feeling miserable for these black bastards. Unless you want to end up like that old hag in the kitchen," Nathanial roared back.

14

Then, realizing he was shouting, he hushed his voice, stepping back to check the stairwell. Nathanial was a large, thick-set man, with a tanned tint to his skin, only hidden by the large, groomed, black beard and sideburns, earned from years at sea in the new West Indies. His height, build and deep commanding voice gave him an instant confidence —one not to be questioned. Years of commanding his own fleet had made him a powerful man, and with this he had a commanding natural authority over people.

The whispering from the other side of the wall was now turning into a mantra, as more voices began joining in. Each sound muffled, giving it a more sinister tone. Faster now, the voices united, stronger and louder, shrieking. Then it ceased, as once more a lone, staring eye peered out at the two men. A child's voice, a young boy, began citing a whispered warning in a strange tongue, his brilliant white teeth grinning at them as they took in what the youngster said. Both men faced each other with disturbed, puzzled expressions. Then they turned back to the wall, fixated on the hole. The smiling mouth, the owners' perfect, white teeth, was clear to see in the dim light.

Leandro stuck the last brick into the wall, placing it into the cement, doing as asked of him. Then he plastered the cement around the brick, sealing the fate of his prisoners. His hands were bleeding from his torn and broken nails, where he had been rushing the work. Then he stood back, glad that it was now finished, so he could get out of the room. His companion stepped forward to check the wall. He tapped it twice, brushing the cement. He wanted to make sure the work was as robust as he hoped.

"Do you not think it was odd?" Leandro asked him. "They never cried out or tried to escape. Not even trying to push the bricks down. They just accepted what we were doing."

"Where would they go? Only to just get hunted down again. No, they had enough of that back home. These fiends do not think, they just do. That is why they became bloody slaves."

"They never even tried to push it down. I do not understand why they did nothing to protest. It is as if they wanted to be left down here. That youngster, he seems to be, well, happy, that we have done this, Nathaniel. It is not normal, I say."

"Normal," Nathaniel hissed. "It's normal that they took my Anabelle, was it? No, they know what they did, and they know they must pay for it. So, stop this pity you feel for the black devils."

Both men propped the cross against the wall. Nathaniel held his lamp up to appreciate the work they had done. In the delicate glimmer, the teary face of Christ, as he lay in pain upon his cross, became highlighted. Leandro stood back, bumping into his friend once more. *At least someone is weeping,* he thought to himself.

"I assumed they may protest a little. At least, the girls might have wept. That young boy, what do you think he meant? All that chanting; something about Loa."

"Look, just forget about it all. Those slaves were trouble, that boy more so."

They leant against the sturdy doors at the entrance, pushing against the heavy metal, then sealed the chamber, leaving the room in blackness. They then bolted the doors, one at the top of the door, one more at the bottom, both clasped by huge brass padlocks.

"Nobody will come down here, that's for sure, and if they do, they won't be getting through that door."

"What about poor Wyn? We cannot just leave her on the kitchen floor?"

Nathaniel Ballard exploded into a rage at the sound of the woman's name. He grabbed his so-called friend by the collar of his sweat-covered shirt, pinning him to the wall of the steps.

"You just do as I say. Do not feel sorry for these peasants, or that sow. I saw her sneaking food to these wretches. Or is it, now, you also feel they were all innocent? It was me who killed Anabelle —is that what you think?"

Leandro prized Nathaniel's hands away from his neck, pushing his deranged friend away. He told him he always took his side and that they were old friends. Nothing had changed.

"Just as well. I need no more deceivers living under my roof."

The two men made their way back to the house, towards the illuminating light in the kitchen window. On the kitchen floor, face down in her own blood, lay the helpless body of Wyn, Ballard's cook. Her head was smashed in by the blood-soaked, heavy pan beside her on the floor.

"She can stay there until the morning. We can sneak her on board the boat."

Leandro was about to protest; he did not agree with the poor woman just lying on the cold, stone floor. Although already dead, he felt she at least deserved dignity. Nathanial noticed his friend stalling at the kitchen table.

"What, do you think better than I do?"

"No, of course not. Come, let us have a deserved drink, my friend, for a job well done."

Leandro knew the offer of a drink would be something his now crazy friend would not refuse. He noticed his friend's drinking had become out of control over the past weeks.

As they walked away from the dead woman, Leandro, with his hand on Nathaniel's shoulder, guiding him away from the kitchen, could not help wonder how long it would be before he suffered a similar fate.

Inside the now tombed room, the slaves assembled in a circle on the stone floor, holding hands. The youngest boy began chanting again. His fellow slaves bent their heads, swaying from side to side in a bizarre rhythm. As if a collective, the circle of slaves looked up, their heads jerked back, glaring into the obscurity, their eyes rolled back, revealing just the whites. Only the young boy remained as he was. The chanting faded away, and the boy looked across at the barricade. In the blackness, he smirked as he sat amongst his followers. Even in their trancelike state, they realized who he was. They always knew, even back in Africa, when the slavers had corralled them together like sheep. Emanuel was the name they gifted him. But to the Vodoun, he was an Iwa, a subservient to the Bondye. His transcendence as a human was unfortunate during the slave trading — it was just poor timing. Yet all this was unrecognized by the white men. As it was by Nathaniel Ballard, even though he seemed unsure about Emanuel, he neglected to see the connection. Only when it was too late would he and his friend, Captain Leandro Fisher RN, learn their mistake. A mistake that would never end for Nathaniel Ballard. The house, the estate he was once so proud of, would never be a peaceful haven again.

As the young slave chanted on, his circle of slaves slumped forward, their life force drained away. Each would create a link into bringing a curse, a demonic entity, that would take Nathanial Ballard's soul, long before he passed away. It would keep him as much a prisoner as the poor Haitian slaves entombed behind the wall.

CHAPTER 1

The weather was turning fast. What little blue sky there was, now seemed to be descending into the solemn greyness of a forthcoming storm.

Justyna struggled to light a cigarette; the breeze, whirling down the stairs from the open deck upstairs, making it difficult. She opened her coat to get protection from the breeze, striking the lighter three times, her icy fingers eventually making a spark. She inhaled hard, dragging on the cigarette, feeling the wave of relief flow through her body, helping her to feel relaxed. As she exhaled, she noticed the 'no smoking' sign on the wall next to her. It had been a painful month for her. She continued smoking. Who was there to reprimand her in this shitty weather, anyway? Even in this inhospitable environment, it felt good to get away. This was a fresh opportunity, the chance to put the last few weeks behind her. If she wanted to smoke, she was going to do so.

Justyna had found out her partner had been cheating on her. This alone was distressing enough, but she had also discovered that he had been spending their savings on his secret affair, convincing her he was away on business trips. Lies were never a good thing in any relationship. Cheating was just too much for her to accept. When she confronted him, he had gone into a frenzy, screaming at her, declaring it was her fault. He said she was cold; she drank too much, and her friends hated him. Which may have been true. In fact, it was true. They never liked him. They always told her she could do so much better. She chose not to listen; you loved who you loved. No, it was none of that; the lies were bad, the cheating worse. For Justyna, any hope that they could fix these, ended because he had hit her. Not a light tap, mind. He full on slapped her across the face, knocking her to the floor. While she was still in a state of shock, he grabbed her by the throat, pulling her to her feet, then pushed her against the wall, screaming at her, saying she was holding him back.

Taking a last draw on the Marlboro, she dropped it on the floor, crushing it with her shoe. She pulled the hood of her coat up. As the icy wind swept around her, Justyna closed her eyes, leaning her head against the iron wall, the material of the hood giving a little softness from the solid wall. She remembered the look in his eyes. He was not even sorry he hit her. He just glared at her, taunting her. It was clear he expected her to retaliate. There was no thought of retaliation. Even with the first shock, she knew it was over. Time to go her own way.

Justyna knew he would never leave the flat. It was his parents' flat. No way was he going to let her win that from him. Besides, what grounds or right did she have to claim it? He was against getting married. Nor did she wish to remain there now, not knowing if he had ever invited his slut back, having been fucking in their bed. No, she had to get out; she did not want to deal with images like that. So, she just waited for him to go to work, gathered her things and left to stay with a friend. Not her best friend, just a close one; someone he was not familiar with, so he could not follow her, though she doubted he would.

Her friend had seen a job posted online, down on the south coast. One hotel was closing for the winter, looking for a housekeeper/caretaker type of role. The Chine Hotel was an old summer retreat, set just off the National Trust land at Studland Bay. It was set in beautiful grounds near the gorgeous beaches of Dorset; a little isolated in the winter, but perfect for her now. The hotel looked like a well-preserved Victorian building. It had extensive panoramic grounds leading to an exclusive beach, along with a charming garden at the front. It seemed idyllic. They needed someone to look after it over the winter closing. To her bewilderment, they offered her the job within hours of her applying online. It was a logical choice for Justyna. A clean start, earn her own money and save while looking for another job throughout the winter months. There was even a full-time offer of work after the winter.

Soon the ferry began berthing, the rattling of the chains resounding across the desolate little harbour once more. The chains jerked the ferry, dragging it around level to let the ramp fall onto the slope. As the shift in direction began, the waves crashed into the side of the ferry, spilling into the stairwell. Justyna jumped up, grabbing her case as the spray invaded her hiding place. Heavy rain blackened the sky; wind was sweeping icy droplets across the beach, mixing with the uplifted sand. It made it hard to see. She rushed through the walkway, making her way down the ramp past the beachfront, her hood pulled down over her forehead. Forced to keep her head down as the sand whipped up within the wind, stinging her face, Justyna followed the path along the side of the road, keeping her eyes on the large ferry chains that ran down the side of the path, guiding her along the road. After a brief walk, she came to a sheltered spot in the tree line further along the path. She felt the wind ease a little, being sheltered from the protecting trees.

Justyna put her case down, looking for the minibus she had been told would wait to collect her. It was there, a little further up the road. Rainwater was streaming from her face. Justyna mopped her brow, searching into the distance, making out the writing on the side of the vehicle. She could run for it. What difference did it make? She was already soaking wet. What did she have to lose? Then she noticed the van was driving towards her, the driver flashing his lights. Pulling up beside her, the driver opened the side door, ushering her inside.

"You must be Justyna, my love. Going to the hotel, I believe?" he asked.

Stepping inside the vehicle, she placed her case on the floor opposite her seat, taking her wet coat off, feeling the warmth of the heaters blowing across the inside of the bus.

"Yes, I am so sorry. It has only been raining for about five minutes. Look at me," she laughed.

"Ah, welcome to Studland. It has its fair share of foul weather. Do not worry about the wet. You get warm. You can sit up here by the heater if you want to get some heat,"

He seemed a nice old boy, with a friendly, strange accent. Must be a local. This was the furthest she had been south. This was how they all spoke. She climbed around the seat at the front, warming her hands in front of the heater vent. He turned up the heating for her. Hunched over, closer to the vents, she felt the warmth taking effect. Justyna thanked him as she put her belt on. The driver turned the minibus around, did a perfect three-point turn, and they were on their way.

Justyna guessed the driver was in his late fifties, dressed in bright-yellow waterproofs. He looked prepared for this weather. His grey hair was not long, yet in need of a haircut. His face was that of an outside worker, tanned even at this time of the year, and it looked fresh. Justyna watched him as he drove. His hands, thick and solid, proved he was a manual worker.

After they were on their way, he introduced himself. "I'm Martin. I am the maintenance manager. Well, I say manager; it is only me. Gardener, driver,

24

whatever, really. They do like to have titles, don't they? Dogsbody, more like."

"Thanks for picking me up. It seems a bit out in the wilderness here," Justyna replied.

"That will be down to the Trust land. We are smack in the middle of that. Never a better spot for a hotel. I would say look around you, not that you can see much in this weather. You get deer in the garden, mind; foxes too. Badgers and birds you will not see elsewhere. But then, look, you get this too. Got to take the rough with the smooth."

"Do you get snow here too, or is it just this rain and wind?"

"Snow, oh, we get snow," he laughed. "Do not you worry about that; we get more than our fair share of snow. Now, it is a lovey place to be and work. Being alone here, well, that is different. You are a braver girl than most."

"If this is when you say it is haunted, it is fine. I have no belief in ghosts. There is always an explanation for them. Is it haunted then?"

"Haunted." He paused. "People do say it, not that I ever saw anything. It is big, and I suppose when it is silent at night, the building will breathe. Now, you put that out of your head. Remember, it is an ancient building, so things go bump in the night. That will just be the enormous rats," he said, smiling across at her.

They held each other's stare, then they both laughed.

"You will be fine, my girl. If it gets too much for you, and something goes tits up, I am a call away — that and a forty-five-minute drive — but you will be OK. Did they not tell you anything about the old building, then?"

She wiped the condensation off the window, looking out. All that was visible was a dark, grey landscape. What scenery there was, was hidden by the downpour. The minibus sped along the little country track, meandering along, passing the open dunes. Soon the dunes became replaced by open heathland. Shadows of the far-away forest stood out like a dark barrier on the distant horizon, blocking the view further. She did not see any attraction to the area.

"No, just that I had the job. That was all they said."

"Well, remember, it is an old but lovely building. On your own, it is different. Just be sure you know what you are taking on. No shame in saying, 'Sorry it is not for me.' But you do have old John."

"So, haunted then. By old John, I take it."

"Ghosts, old stories and these old buildings go hand in hand, going back generations. Saying that, you will not get me staying there into the late evening. Old John is no ghost, my girl. He be the best rum money can buy."

"Why, are you scared of the hotel?" she mocked her new friend.

"You may well laugh, my girl. Not scared, no. I just dislike the fact of being alone in it, even with two or three nips of Old John."

Justyna left it there, being too cold and wet to consider what he was on about. Haunted or not, she never believed in such things, nor had she any interest to converse about it.

The van turned off the road, into a landscaped garden, twisting and turning along the tarmacked drive that led to the front of The Chine. Justyna saw the hotel appearing out of the rain. Even through the rain it looked big, yet ancient. It was three floors high, with a tower at each end, offering panoramic views. Enormous pine trees were scattered around the edge of the grounds, their thick, dark branches twisted and reaching out to the hotel, as if they were trying to stretch out to touch the building. They all were the same height, with thick trunks. They gave the hotel a canopy as they stretched around the grounds. The brown, brick structure was broken up by white and black beams that were crisscrossing the middle of the building between each floor. It had been designed with a Tudor look. Along the high roof were large, brick, chimney stacks, all at various heights and shapes. Rain was pouring off the roof, flooding over the guttering. A square, white, arch-covered entrance, that looked a little more modern — obviously added later — had "The Chine" etched across the sides in bold, black letters.

Justyna leant forward, looking out at The Chine, thinking that the hotel seemed natural, placed in the secluded grounds, yet somehow it seemed out of place.

As if it had been dropped into the scenery. Justyne could imagine it having been the house of a rich family once.

The painted lower floor of the building was illuminated by blue, neon lights from spaced-out ground spotlights. It seemed, with the rain hindering the projection, that the hotel had a weird half-light effect. The larger windows had outdoor balconies overlooking the gardens. On either side of the third floor were two large tower structures, each circled by a larger balcony stretching around the towers. This must be where the bigger, more expensive, suites were found, Justyna thought. All under a brown-tiled roof.

Justyna considered it would be a picturesque retreat in the warmer seasons. Even in this foul weather, she understood the idea of coming here at the height of summer.

Martin pulled up, ushering her inside, saying he would bring her case once he parked. Justyna made her way inside the hotel, her coat over her head shielding her from the now torrential rain blowing across the gardens.

The receptionist was waiting to greet her: a thin, well-dressed, middle-aged lady; well-spoken with no notable accent. Her hair was tied in a tight bun, not one strand out of place.

She introduced herself and welcomed Justyna, saying they were expecting her. The woman took her coat, violently shaking it to her side and flicking the rain from it, before draping it across one of the sofas. She showed her to a comfortable seat next to the radiator, offering her a fresh pot of coffee. She informed Justyna the manager would be with her very soon, as there were no guests in the hotel. Justyna watched her as she made her way back behind the reception desk. She was tall, slim and dressed in a stylish, yet dated uniform. Strict — a no-nonsense type, Justyna thought.

Sat in the sparsely lit, oak-panelled lobby, Justyna clocked her surroundings. Deep-varnished oak panels adorned the walls throughout the lobby. Justyna guessed they could be the original fittings. Large oil paintings of stern-looking men from a long time ago, stared down upon her, making her feel a little uncomfortable. A violent shiver shot through her body. She rubbed her arms and shoulders, searching for warmth, wishing the coffee would hurry and arrive.

It seemed a little dark for a hotel lobby, Justyna thought, as she began looking up at the chandelier set high in the ceiling, noting it only had half the bulbs lit. It gave the lobby a gloaming appearance, and with the creepy, old men portraits, it was even spooky. Lights flickered from the lone Christmas tree set in the far corner of the lobby. Colours casting across the walls were enhanced by the polished wood surroundings. They highlighted the faces in the paintings, which seemed to burst into life every time the brighter illuminating lights danced across them. Were they judges or something, with their odd hairstyles? Important people, she guessed, squinting and examining the paintings. Not the style of paintings that she liked. Yet she found it hard to look away from them. Why did they look so angry? They seemed upset with her. She felt a shiver run through her bones again. She forced herself to look away, thinking it weird that the hotel had decorated the hotel lobby with these odd, grumpy characters. Weirder was the fact that the only decoration showing that it was Christmas, was the lone tree. Not another decoration anywhere.

Her mind was all over the place. Did it matter that the hotel closed for the festive period? She was overthinking things again. She should not of drank the bottle of wine first thing this morning. Old paintings were normal in old hotels like The Chine.

They drew her back, though. Justyna felt they were watching her. Those clever paintings where the eyes follow you around the room. Was she still a little drunk? She made an excuse to herself that she was nervous. The wine was only for liquid courage, nothing to do with being drunk. She had drunk wine first thing in the morning before, when she was nervous. This job would get her out of trouble. Leaving her asshole boyfriend was a godsend. Plus, it was a chance to have somewhere to live over the Christmas period. She had no problem being alone in such a large hotel, having stayed in far worse places in her time. This chance would help her to save some money, then plan her next job. They may even keep her on. She wished she never opened that bottle of merlot now. Drawn back to the paintings, examining them, they were beginning to look threatening now.

"Ah, wigs." Her voice echoed through the empty room, causing the woman at the reception desk to look up.

"Sorry, did you say something?"

"No, well, yes, I was admiring the paintings. Are they famous people?"

"I do not know; I do not think so. They creep me out, the way they follow you around the room," she said.

She never even looked up from her desk to see what Justyna was enquiring about. It was obviously something that had been asked before.

Justyna moved her head from side to side, checking that out. She was not sure. Sitting down did not help. They just were staring at her. So, she decided the less she knew about the creepy, old men, the better. If she were to stay here alone over winter, she did not need to know whose eyes were following her around the lobby. She decided that as soon as she was alone, she would turn them around to face the wall. Who would know?

Just then the sound of footsteps took her attention away, as a man appeared, dressed in a stylish, blue suit. As he approached her, he offered his hand. She shook his hand, standing up to introduce herself.

"Nice to meet you, Justyna, I am so sorry to keep you waiting. How was the journey? The Chine is a little way off the mainland. The ferry is fine if you work nine to five. For us lot, it is often the long, country road back to the actual world, as it stops running at ten p.m."

He introduced himself as Rob Greensmith, general manager of The Chine. He was an older man — older that the receptionist — not overweight, but he was a little chubby around the middle. He was slightly balding, and although he was well spoken and educated, he did seem very on edge and nervous. He kept looking up at the portraits as he placed his hand on the small of Justyna back, ushering her into his office behind the reception. He introduced Megan, his reception manager.

As they sat down in the little office, he poured her a coffee, which she gladly accepted. Justyna felt the hot drink warm her in seconds. She was glad to feel the chill in her body subside, as they discussed the role.

He explained his role, and the one he expected her to fulfil while the hotel closed. He explained a few vital actions they expected Justyna to do. She was always to keep the hotel locked. The rear doors of the hotel all had a barred outer gate. All doors were to remain locked, as were the ground-floor kitchen windows. The hotel CCTV was to be on constantly. She was to change the tapes daily at twelve noon. The number of the maintenance manager was on the board, as well as the number of the local police, and other emergency numbers.

"We do have an issue with the CCTV. It sometimes sticks or freezes, but as long as the tapes are changed, the insurance agents cannot complain, can they?" he joked, and continued, "We are all a fair way away. I will be in the west country. However, should you need me for any emergency, call our maintenance chap, Martin. He will come if it is an emergency, nothing more. He will be here later to run through the boiler and heating for you, plus any other duties, of course."

"I am sure I will be fine, if he walks me through the lighting and the heating. They say we are in for a cold, wet winter out here," Justyna said.

"We are, but you will be perfectly safe." He paused, looking around. "Well, safe here, I am sure of it, if you support the important rules about security. Not that it is a dangerous place — far from it. This is a beautiful place in the summer. Guests come and go, yet, in the winter, there are never many bookings, because of the weather you see. The wind from the sea is bitter and sharp. It rains or snows. So it's better to close for a couple of months."

She was sure he was nervous of something, but she decided not to push him on it, this being her first day. They worked through the rules and health and safety regulations, and all the normal day-to-day things Justyna needed to know. After they consumed the coffee, he proposed he show her around the hotel.

"We can start downstairs, then I can show you the bedrooms. May I recommend you accept one of the tower suites, as they have a nice lounge space, full TV coverage, and the most marvellous views across the grounds. Of course, the appeal is the beautiful view of the beaches. Oh, and the most lavish of Jacuzzi baths."

She appreciated the sound of that. A bath right now would be bliss. Justyna followed him through the carpeted hall into the hotel lounge. The view overwhelmed her. They had renovated the lounge to a significant standard. In the corner was a grand piano. They had mounted an enormous stag's head on the far wall, above a massive granite fireplace. It was the hugest fire she had ever seen.

"Yes, that is the authentic fire from the original house, long before the hotel days. This used to be the estate owners original home long ago. Remarkable piece."

"Very nice, but I will have to take your word on that, as all I saw was the rain. Will I be able to light it and sit down here reading in the evenings?" she enquired.

Justyna tried to figure out where his accent came from. She wasn't sure if it was an accent. Perhaps the sign of a good private education. He seemed posh and well groomed.

"Of course, I will make sure Martin leaves you a good deal of wood. I expect you will find sitting here could be very relaxing. The view into the garden is very serene. We even have deer foraging at the bottom of the garden in the late evenings. Then again, you would be just as comfortable and safe staying in your room."

Justyna looked up at the stag, feeling that his remark was satirical. Mr Greensmith laughed, recognizing what she was assuming.

"Perhaps they realize he is up there, hence they never move to close, eh," she mocked

Moving on, he took her into the bar, a snug, dimly lit room, with blood-red chesterfield furniture evenly spaced around the room, each with its own table. You could detect the bouquet of leather in the air, from where they had polished the cushions. The long, oak-topped bar counter highlighted the room. Behind the bar was a multitude of diverse whiskeys and rums, all shelved. A lack of bar seats showed that this was a bar where the guests sat and relaxed. It wasn't a place to sit at the bar, getting drunk. The brands they had on display were the leading end of the spirit brands. Justyna noted the decanter's Macallan and a bottle of Royal Brackla. Not cheap at all. There, as Martin had said, sat a large, plain bottle, with the name 'Old John' on it. Not that she was a whisky expert, though she knew what a good spirt was. She did have a taste for spiced rum.

Justyna had found employment with the Fairmont group for four years and had found herself working in Hawaii at the prestige Orchid Hotel. Head-hunted later, she was promoted to front of house manager at the luxurious Hamilton Princess Beach Club in Bermuda. So she was aware of what top-end products were. But this was a brand she never heard of before.

"I see you have quite a selection. Old John is new to me," she said.

"Ah, yes, extremely popular it is, too. Made in a local bar on the mainland. I am not one for spirits, of any form, though I hear that this brand is, as I say, immensely popular."

Then he was ushering her out of the bar, nervously looking around as if they were trespassing. Justyna thought back to something he had said in the lounge, about staying in her room. Odd; the more she thought about it, the more it was a request, rather than a suggestion.

"Justyna, use the bar stock within reason. I do not expect you to be here for Christmas, drinking tea. I do not think for a second you will deplete the stock, though. Please try to control the intake to the normal levels. This is not a place to be alone and drunk."

"Oh, of course. I am not a huge drinker," she lied.

Greensmith's tone had changed to a sort of whisper when he mentioned being alone, as if he was telling her a secret. He paused, placing his hand on her shoulder. His face looked sincere, peering around, as if people were listening in. "Excellent. Besides, who knows what that would do to your imagination."

"No, I can imagine how that would be. I may have a glass of wine with dinner," she lied again.

"Of course. If you feel you would like one of your friends to stay over, do. It might be a comfort for you, as being alone here can be, well, strange. I am not averse to that at all, but just drop a message to let us know — insurance laws and all that."

Justyna was sure he seemed concerned about something. Was he warning her about drinking the stock or was it a hint about what her imagination would see? He seemed skittish, glancing around. Justyna was not sure if he was just looking at everything for security reasons; checking that everything was ready for the closure — locked, all in place. Or was he searching for something else, someone else, something else?

The tour continued into the sales and accounts office, and then down into the kitchen where he pointed out that the fridges were well stocked. The chef had made a range of meals for her from the restaurant menu. They were placed in a large freezer for her to select. There was more than enough food for her to make use of. He showed her the cooker she could use. They had made sure she would want for nothing during her stay. She felt pleased with how organized they had been on her behalf.

The tour continued upstairs to the rooms. They skipped the lower floors, as the rooms were double and single. Taking her to the tower suite, Greensmith showed her into the room he had informed her about earlier. It was very pleasant; she felt it would be ideal for her. The lounge had a nice, soft double sofa, and a large armchair was placed at the window where you could sit looking out across the gardens. You could see the sea away in the distance.

The warm pastel colours of the walls gave the room warmth. Large double doors led into the bedroom to reveal a huge king-size bed. She had to resist the urge to run and jump on it; it looked that comfortable. The room felt warm and had lots of storage place.

Justyna noted that Martin had brought her case up to the room. Seeing it placed on the rug at the side of the bed made her feel like she had run away. Was that all she had in the world — one suitcase full of clothing? For a second, she felt she should have stayed at the flat. Then she dismissed that idea. No, he could drop dead. She felt nothing for him. The only thing she missed were her souvenirs from around the world. She felt she was going to be OK here. It seemed the right thing for her.

The tour over, they made their way back down to his office. Both parties asked and answered questions. Soon they were back in his office, going through bank details and confirming that everything was correct.

"Can I inquire why you chose this hotel, Justyna? With your accomplishments, you could be anywhere in the world. Your references are spot on. You're young and charming. Would a job in the sun not suit your experience further?" Greensmith challenged her.

"Yes. I have done that; it is an excellent climate to work in. I just need to get away — revise my home life. It all went, let me just say, crashing down," she responded, looking to suppress her regret.

"I see — man troubles. We are not the best partners sometimes. Well, his loss is our gain. I am sure that, if you feel it is for you, I can find a management role here for you when we open again. That was the reason I acknowledged you so hastily — you would be ideal for our guests."

"It would thrill me, Rob, thank you very much."

"Right, we can talk about that another time. I should thank you for taking the role to look after The Chine. It is not everyone's cup of tea. I mean, being alone here over the winter. So, do you have any questions for me?"

"You said 'safe' when you mentioned my room. I'd be safe in my room, you said."

Martin knocked on the door, carrying in a tray with a bottle of his famous rum and four glasses. Megan came in with him. Rob Greensmith just smiled at Justyna, happy he never had to answer her question.

"Come on, time to offer the girl a proper refreshment, since we're the last people she will see for a while. What better time to introduce her to Old John."

Caramel scent filled the office as they all shared the warming drink. They each offered Justyna the best of luck, to relax and enjoy the peace.

Megan thought to herself about her house being full over the festive holiday. She would get no rest, running around after her in-laws, though she would rather have that than stay in The Chine over the festive period.

She asked Justyna if there was anything she needed to know before they left for the ferry. Greensmith bid her farewell as Megan hugged her, telling her she would see her in the new year, leaving Martin to take her through the heating system, which keys she would need, how to set the alarm system, and all the smaller details, even where the log store was.

"I have stockpiled logs in the fire's hearth for you. That will keep you from having to go outside for a few days, collecting wood."

"That is kind of you, Martin, thank you. I think everything will be fine. I am good with my own company, and the TV will have lots of films on — repeats, I expect. Still, I am looking forward to just chilling out for a change."

"I will say this: remember, it is an old hotel. It will creak and moan, you know that. Should you go for a walk in the grounds, try not to look up at the windows; your mind can play tricks on you. Shadows from the clouds, flushing across the glass; wind sneaking in the cracks in the frames. All can perform tricks on your mind, my girl. So just do not get spooked by something that you think you have seen."

"Of course. I do not believe in ghosts, Martin. Besides, if the weather stays like this, I will be inside all the time," she responded, laughing.

"You got the snow to come yet; that will give the place a Christmas card look. It will charm you, trust me."

"I bet cold, too, Martin," Justyna joked.

"Oh, aye, that it will be. Try that Old John; it will warm you, whatever the temperature is. The old boy will never know."

"Can you tell me anything more about the hotel — its history or beginnings? Just out of curiosity," Justyna asked.

"Of course. Well, what I know, that is," Martin replied.

He looked around, as if he were looking for anyone listening; as if he were about to explain a secret.

"This was a private estate — all the land, the house, everything. It was given to the Purifoy family, for helping them support the transport of sugar. They were something big about shipping in the Caribbean, though this was all a cover, as they were more interested in the transporting of slaves. As the colonies' crops often failed, it scattered the regions with jobless vagrants and beggars, picked up and made to work the plantations or sent to British colonies as punishment. Then somewhere down the line, they found it easier, or cheaper, to transport slaves."

"That is awful. How did they get away with that?"

"Ah, a bloody lot of the wealthy aristocracy had become involved in slavery, kept hidden from the world. That kind of money commands power. Families mixed in politics. Sons and uncles all had important posts in the government. Estates were cropping up across the country. They put money into forestry, farming and property. All the wealth from slaves. Making money from human misery."

"I knew slavery existed, but not on home soil. Were they a bad family, then?"

"Oh, yes. Having their own land and their own hidden harbour, it was easy to land his booty on his own shore. Yet, he mistreated his slaves — beatings, even torture. Yet to his own kind, he was a great man. Sir Nathaniel Ballard — a great merchant trader of the day. Who knew the horrors he carried out."

"Wow, and the family today are happy with their history. I do not think I would be happy knowing my family were slavers. How did the Chine become a hotel? Did he lose it all?" Justyna asked.

"I do not think so. I heard that the family had no male heir, so the family divided the land. They left this old house empty. The family built a new estate in the middle of the forestry area, more arable for farming. They tried to sell this place, but nobody wanted it. So, it was decided that, due to the area being as it is, it be converted into a country hotel. Not all the family were fortunate over the years; it took time to get back the respect. I hear rumours that there is still a riff in the family. The eldest boy refuses to be part of the family. Then the National Trust took over the land, as it was a natural preservation area. That is all I know."

"All? That is a fair bit of knowledge, Martin. You could be a tourist guide."

Martin laughed, explaining he was born and bred in the area, declaring that he grew up with the local myths and legends. He added he had been working at The Chine since he left school, as did his father before him, and his father before that. It was a family tradition of sorts, he told her.

"Any local knows the story of the region," he said.

If someone looked deep enough, dark history would become known to all, he explained. Laughing, they wandered through the hotel. Everything was clarified and understood. Justyna escorted him to the front of the hotel where they bid goodbye, and he got in his car, driving off. As he drove away, he glanced back at her in his rearview mirror, watching her waving farewell to him. He exhaled, as if he had been holding it in. Martin hoped she would feel safe, even though he knew she would not, feeling that if she never believed in ghosts, they would leave her alone. He never really believed that, though. As he drove away, he could feel that eyes were already watching.

Closing the big, wooden doors and locking them, Justyna went straight to the bar and poured herself a straight shot of the spiced rum, as recommended. The warm, caramel sweetness was intense, the aftertaste of the rum lingering. She took a pint glass and added a double measure, topping it up with coke from the soft drink syphon. After the first sip, Justyna began relaxing. She felt relieved they had gone. She liked them all,

Martin more so. He seemed a nice guy, concerned for her.

She made her way back to the lounge. As she walked along the hallway, she looked at the portraits along the walls. They were all edged with old-fashioned, bold frames, identically and evenly placed along the hallway. They were large oil paintings, showing the surrounding coastline along with various shipwrecks and landmarks. Each showed various aspects of the land, expertly painted, and colourful. Each offered a unique view of the county coastline.

Hung in the centre of the hallway, opposite the restaurant, was a portrait of a young woman. Unsmiling, yet attractive, her dark hair draped across bare shoulders. Justyna leant closer, noticing that over the years the oil had begun to crack faintly. It gave the women in the portrait a frail look. She seemed sad, her eyes a little darker than they should have been.

Justyna stepped back as she checked her image in the glass's reflection. Her hair was a mess. The rain had made her look dishevelled. She ran her fingers through her long, blonde curls. That jacuzzi was looking like a terrific offer now. She walked away towards the lounge. Her reflection in the glass of the framed picture was now gone, yet, replacing her dishevelled, wet look, there now stared out an elderly lady. Her pale, white features matched her powder-white, untidy hair, floating around her as if windswept. Dark eyes, devoid of colour, looked back at the unsuspecting Justyna, watching her walking away down the hallway. Then she faded, as the image of the original portrait returned.

CHAPTER 2

Martin had set the fire up, making it easier for Justyna to light. She smirked to herself, delighted that he had done so. The fire soon caught, and flames from pine logs flickered across the wood, crackling as it overwhelmed the wood. A sweet bouquet of pine filled the area in an instant. A big, warm fire would give her a comfort of sorts for the coming wintry nights.

Justyna sat in the seat by the fire. It had become dark outside now. Rain clouds, dark and threatening, had now diminished any light from the afternoon sky. The light from the fire was casting shadows across the lounge. Justyna watched the fire burn, almost hypnotized by the dancing flames. By adding more logs to the hearth, she made sure it would burn well into the night.

Sat back in the comfortable chair, she drank her rum & coke. She decided she should call her friends, letting them know she had arrived and how charming it was at the hotel. She seemed relaxed, for once, happy that she had made the right decision. She called her best friend.

"Guess where… no, guess *what* I am doing," she challenged Adyta.

"If I know you, maybe seated in the bar, reducing their stock."

"No, cheeky. I am sitting in front of the most enormous fire. Feet up, and yes, with an amazing drink, feeling warm and cosy. The whole hotel to myself."

"Alone already, wow. I thought they would stick around with you for a day or so. Why did they leave you so soon? Is it haunted?" Adyta laughed.

"Who cares if it is haunted? Come on down, you would love it. It is old, though. They left straight away. They sounded nice, though. The manager walked me around the building. The chef has made me a shitload of classy dinners. I can even drink from the bar if I wish to. Pretty cool, eh."

"I bet he wouldn't say that if he knew you could drink most people under the table."

"Adyta, it is a pleasant hotel. Big, a little out of the way, middle of nowhere. But the area is stunning. Well, they say it is. I cannot tell, as it was pissing down on the way here, though Martin said it is a wonderful place to work."

"Martin? Who is this, then? You hooked up already?" Adyta was teasing her.

"Adyta, he must be about sixty-five, but still an improvement on John," she giggled.

"Are you sure? You will be a prisoner in that hotel for the winter. It sounds too solitary for you."

"It will be fine. I have the whole place to myself, and I can go out if I want. The grounds are incredible. It's cold. I guess, when it snows, it will be warmer."

"Snow; since when did you like snow? You lived in the sun for god knows how long."

"Look, I will be OK. I have Old John," Justyna replied.

"Who? You're not alone then?" Adyta asked

"Relax. Old John is the local rum, and I must say, it is so nice, I think it will replace my whisky days."

The two went on. Justyna told her all about the hotel, from what she knew so far: her room, the jacuzzi, not neglecting to point out the bar stock and all the expensive spirits she had yet to try over her first-class dinners. They promised to stay connected. Justyna was to call her the minute she felt lonely.

After disconnecting the call, Justyna went to draw the lounge drapes. They were long, patterned drapes that reached from the top of the windows down to the floor. Then she stood behind them, peering out into the hotel grounds. The rain had eased off, now just a slight drizzle, the sky as black as coal. The hotel gardens looked sombre and mystical in the dark. She could just make out the tree line at the bottom of the garden. She placed her drink on the windowsill. Cupping her hands to her face, she pressed her hands to the glass, peering out into the gloom. She saw nothing. Why would she? It was just her here now. What sort of idiot would be out in this weather?

The wind was whistling around the building, constructing a variety of wailing pitches. Justyna picked her drink up, consuming the liquid in glass. Time for another, she thought, then a hot bath. She looked at her reflection in the glass once more. She looked a mess. She wondered what the staff must have thought of her, looking like a drenched rat. Still, they seemed none too concerned with her appearance.

She looked back into the garden, listening to the wind. In an instant, she was falling backwards, reaching out for the drapes to support her. A falling branch from the pine tree smashed against the glass, hitting it with an almighty bang, causing her tired legs to give way, her heart racing in a sudden fit of shock. She dropped her glass as she fell.

"Jesus Christ," she shouted out, the pulse of her racing heartbeat pounding in her ears. She sat in a heap on the floor, with the end of the curtains draped over her head.

For some odd reason, she looked around, embarrassed, peering from under the drapes as if someone may have seen her. Swearing aloud, she pulled herself to her feet and closed the drapes again. Feeling cold, she walked back to the fireplace and stood in front of the fire. Folding her arms, she rubbed her shoulders, looking back across at the drapes. She shook her head in disbelief at her fright.

"Just a branch, Justyna, it was just a branch," she said out loud.

She needed a bath and a drink. Justyna retrieved the empty glass from the floor at the base of the drapes. Then she made her way back through the lobby, heading back to the bar. After a quick glance over the wines on the rack, Justyna took a red Shiraz, then made her way up the stairs, to her room, for a welcome bath.

Outside in the rear garden, the wind was picking up, forming a whirlwind of fallen leaves dancing across the lawns. In the tree line, the sparks of a lighter broke the blackness from just inside the trees. A wisp of smoke flowed away into the breeze. A lone figure was watching as the tower room lights lit up the corner of the hotel, then diminished as Justyna lowered the blinds. Leaning against the pine tree, the figure had been observing Justyna's actions, amused at her frightening issue with the branch. The glow of the cigarette butt shot through the night as the smoker flipped it away into the wind. He stepped back into the trees and walked away into the woodland.

Justyna unpacked her case as her bath ran, the steam flowing out of the bathroom into the lounge. She stood nude, looking into the fitted mirrors on the wardrobes opposite the bed. She studied herself, spinning one way then the other. At thirty, she looked good, just under six feet. Her hair was that of a natural strawberry-blonde-haired person. Her figure was curvy and respectable; not model slim, yet a long way from being overweight. Cupping her breasts, she studied them; a nice size — firm and shapely. Her waist matched her hips and bust. She took a deep breath, holding it as she pondered her reflection. She was happy with her slender legs and toned calves. Never using cheap makeup, she never went over the top; just adequate to feature her bone structure. She was attractive, so she never needed a great deal of makeup. It was harsh to tolerate that her ex had looked elsewhere, finding another woman. Not that Justyna felt she had failed. It was more a mixture of betrayal and trust. She looked happy with her looks and proud of who she was. No more trying for him. Time for herself. Push him out of her head. It was his loss, not hers. She was glad she got out. All the offers she had wasted because she was a loyal companion.

She strutted model style into the bathroom, one foot in front of the other, her glass of wine in hand. She dipped her toe into the hot, steamy bath, the windows and mirror steaming up as the heat from the water filled the room. She sunk down until her shoulders were covered, struggling to keep her glass out of the water.

She started singing, "I'm going to wash that man right out of my hair," as the warmth swept across her. She placed her glass down on the surface beside her. She hit the water-jet button. The water churned to life. The reverberation was an extra enjoyment for her.

She thought back, laughing to herself at the fright earlier. She guessed she should get used to sudden bangs and bumps like that in a hotel of this age and size, since it was empty. Creaks and bumps would be normal. She felt much more at ease now. The wine helped.

Closing her eyes, she imagined how her Christmas would be on her own. She did not know how long she had been in the bath, as it was not long before she began drifting off into a daydream. Yet the water still had a fair amount of heat in it, so it was not too long. Her arms on the side of the bath, she pushed herself up to get out. She slipped on a bathrobe and towel-dried her hair. She locked her bedroom door then clambered into the enormous bed, tugging the duvet up to her chin. She reached out to the bedside table. She picked up the bottle of wine, drinking straight from the bottle. Then, placing it back, she closed her eyes. She fell asleep within minutes.

Throughout the hotel, the dark halls were silent now. In the lobby, the portraits of the three historic men peered down into the room, staring out from the frames. In the lounge, the fire was smouldering a vibrant crimson as the last of the logs burnt down. Behind the large drapes, beyond the glass, the wind had settled down, succeeded by a consistent, light, hazy rain. Only the fire, the embers crackling, gave away a hint of noise. Throughout the hotel, the faint crackle from the log embers echoed through the halls, fading away in the darkness. Each corner of the lounge was lit by the slight radiance of the perishing fire. Reflections of the red embers were mirrored on the black lustre of the open lid of the grand piano. The dying noise of the crackling fire was now replaced by the keys of the piano pressed down in a timed sequence. An invisible, gentle touch drew the piano to life, gliding across the ivory keys, as Ravel's *Pavane pour une infante defunte*, filled the room with a ghostly melody, ebbing away as the fire died. As soon as the music faded away, the sound of laughter filled the room. Not an enjoyable, joyous laugh. This was a deep laughter — sinister, devious. The room went cold, the fire now long gone out. Windows drapes fluttered in the darkness. At the centre of the room, the figure of a man faded in and out of focus. His face was set in half shadow, the eyes darkened against his eerie, transparent, ghostly face. He looked upwards to the ceiling, searching, his ghostly face fading away then reappearing at various areas of the room, as he looked left then right. Swirls of ghostly vapours were the only trace of his movement. Then he disappeared as fast as he had arrived. The room remained cold. The sound of footsteps could be heard, running along the halls in the darkness, running up and down the staircase. Invisible, yet audible. Children's laughter, getting louder, as the footsteps went from one end of the hotel to another. The apparition appeared again, manifesting all over the ground floor, its ghostly face twisted in anger as it searched for children. Not being able to find them, it emitted a deep roar. As the chandeliers shook, the drapes in the lounge fluttered, like capes in the wind, and the room was once more shrouded in a fierce coldness. The children stopped running, and The Chine fell silent once more.

Justyna opened her eyes, staring into the darkness, her brain struggling to take in where she was. Her eyes adjusted to the dark, as she realized where she was. Reaching out from under the duvet, she picked up her phone off the bedside cabinet. She turned it on to check the time. Four thirty. It was still early. Why had she woken up so soon? Justyna was not one to wake up early. In fact, the opposite — she always slept well, not rising until the second alarm forced her to get up. She dropped the phone back on the cabinet, her body shuffling under the duvet to get back into a warm place. Once more she drifted off, hoping she could find the earlier happy dream. As she began to drift off, her mind was searching, trying to recall something. Piano music — Justyna was positive she heard a piano playing. Was someone — a child — laughing? Dismissing it, she fell back to sleep.

Outside, at the other end of the rear gardens, watching from the far end of the grounds, another watcher stood hiding in the dark, sheltering from the elements, on the far side of the pines. He also showed an interest in The Chine and its new guest. He was now aware of the other figure hiding across the other side of the garden. The figure flicked the cigarette into the wind, revealing its presence. The young girl had drawn more attention than was first thought. Someone else had an interest in the woman, or were they watching for

54

something more sinister? Likewise, following suit, the figure turned and walked away into the night, aware of what was happening in The Chine — the laughing and the sound of music from an empty room. This was nothing new to the second mystery figure. It was expected more now than ever. Yet, there was no need to venture closer. Not yet. The orders were to just watch and keep back. Nathaniel Ballard would show himself, or his demon would.

It was past nine a.m. when Justyna woke. She showered, dressed and was soon in the hotel kitchen, making herself breakfast. She was spoilt for choice, being that there was so much to choose from, the hotel chef having set aside one refrigerator for breakfast ingredients. There were kippers, smoked and unsmoked; kedgeree and large catering packs of various bacon; white and black puddings and duck eggs and quail eggs. It was more than she would even consider at home for breakfast. After taking some bread, she slotted them in the large toaster, while she grilled bacon slices along with a little portion of mushrooms. While these cooked, she made a pot of coffee.

Justyna took her food into the large dining room, deciding to choose a window table. She ate her bacon and mushroom, toasted sandwich, all the while looking out across the garden. The previous night's weather had blown an assortment of woodland debris all over the lawn. It lay scattered across the manicured garden, waiting for the coming winds to dump it elsewhere. It seemed calm outside this morning. Cold yet calm.

As she drank her coffee, she wondered what she should do. She felt the heat from the restaurant radiator under the window. She was not sure if she should leave the warmth of the hotel. Maybe light the fire first, so she could come back into a warm lounge.

Yes, that was a great idea. Finish the pot of coffee, have a first smoke of the day, then venture out to look around the hotel. She used the saucer as an ashtray. Since the hotel had a no smoking policy, there was a lack of ashtrays. So the saucer would make do. Besides, who was here to protest she was smoking? It was just her.

As Justyna finished her first smoke, she turned to look around her, her hand wafting the smoke away, leaning back in her chair and stretching. Odd, she thought. There was a strange smell of lavender — modest but present. It played with her senses. It was a familiar perfume — not one that was common — yet it was one she had detected before. She rose and walked around the room, pursuing the origin. It had diminished as fast as it had arrived. She picked her coffee pot up, smelling the spout, as if it had a flavoured aroma. Replacing the pot on the table, Justyna shrugged. Why would the coffee smell of lavender? It was a room odour — a plug-in scent, or something similar.

She gave up and began cleaning her table. She scanned the skirtings as she walked, checking for air fresheners, but she could see no plug-in air fresheners. Weird, she thought to herself. It was lavender she could smell, with no doubt.

The little, old woman sat sipping her tea, her pale hands holding the decorated teacup with dignity. She watched the young girl, from her table at the side of the room, undisturbed by Justyna walking around her table. Justyna was stretching her neck out, investigating the smell in the air as she weaved in and out amongst the tables. As the old lady watched Justyna walk through the restaurant, her pale face tracked her every move. She knew Justyna felt her presence, yet she still refused to admit to herself that she wasn't alone.

Turning back to her table, Justyna paused, her body feeling cold, her breath fog-like as it appeared from her body. Someone was at the table; she could sense it. She never believed in ghosts though, it was absurd. Yet her mind was demanding to confirm her senses. Walking to her own table, she collected her plate, placing her cup onto it. Then she swiftly turned around in the hope she would see something. She felt reassured at seeing no one, yet she still felt the cold and the coldness of her breathing. Once more she scanned the room, as she placed her unoccupied hand onto the cup to stop the shaking.

"Come on, Justyna, don't get jittery on the first day," she whispered to herself.

Returning to the kitchen and setting her things into the sink, she made her way back through the restaurant, heading to the reception area. She passed the table where the old lady had sat. She stopped, shoving the chair back under the table. She was not sure why, but she lay her hand, palm down, on the seat, feeling the warmth, and replayed the action on the next seat. It was cold. Feeling a shiver run through her, she placed the chairs back under the table. Standing and looking out into the garden, her reflection intensified from the lights of the restaurant. Looking back at her in the glass, the old lady was standing beside her, smiling, as they stood side by side. Justyna turned so fast she felt her neck spasm. Peering back to the window and back again around the room, she replayed it over again. She walked back up the small stairs, almost running out of the restaurant entrance. It was then that she noticed the large portrait of the elderly woman on the wall. That was conclusive enough for her. That was what she saw in the window. Yes, she was sure. What else could it have been?

Laughing to herself, she made her way to the reception, replaced the CCTV tapes, marking the day and time of the change. Deep inside her mind, she knew she saw something, or someone. If she dwelled on the matter, it would make her stay at the hotel more of a challenge; more of an awkward, frightening stay. Her solid belief that ghosts were just for movies and stories held. It was then that she realized that the portrait was of a young woman, not an old lady. She froze for a few seconds, trying to figure out what she saw, replaying her steps over and over, her head turning as if she was seeing her actions in her mind. Stood at the window restaurant, she saw an old woman. Of course not. How stupid was she? She would think no further on the event — it was just a trick of the light.

So she continued. Turning the hotel sound system on, she filled the lobby and lounge with music; not too loud — just enough to keep the areas lively. Then, making a fresh coffee from the office Tassimo machine, she went to light the fire. Once again, she passed the glaring portraits in the lobby. This time, she noticed the small brass plates at the bottom of the frames. She read the names aloud. "Nathaniel Ballard. Head of the Estate."

Justyna looked up at him. It was hard to figure how old he was in the portrait. He must have been in his forties, at least. He looked overweight. A huge mane of frizzy hair draped down past his shoulders. He wore a long, black overcoat with lace collar and sleeves, and funny embroidered leggings, and buckled shoes. To Justyna, he looked angry about something. Yes, he seemed important, but he did not seem like he was an approachable sort of man. Next to him, the other portrait said, 'Captain Leandro Fisher, RN'. Another oddly dressed man, nothing like how she imagined a naval officer to dress. His face was flushed red under a very fluffed-up hairdo, again, reaching down past his shoulders. His uniform was a brilliant royal blue, full of golden stripes and buttons. He held a long telescope, it seemed. Again, the portrait held a cold, unhappy look. Justyna considered that was how they were in those days. She was sure she read somewhere that, in earlier centuries, they never smiled in portraits, looking as menacing as possible.

They were all friends. There was no resemblance to show they could be family — that, and the names were all different. The other one had no name plate, though they all dressed alike — simply good friends.

She reminded herself to turn them around to face the wall, later in the day, as they just seemed so miserable, their eyes following her every time she passed them.

Fire lit, she walked to the garden window, looking out as the first of the snow fell, covering the garden in a pure white blanket. Thick flakes drifted down across the rear of the hotel as the wind dropped. The trees now looked like a scene from the front of a Christmas card.

Coffee finished, Justyna looked out across the garden, deciding she would look from her room, wanting to see the view from a higher point. She put a cigarette into her mouth. Picking up a large splinter from one log, she poked the thin end into the fire, taking a light from the glowing wood. She popped into the bar, searching around the shelves. Finding a small, silver, Jack Daniel's hip flask, she filled it with Old John, taking a quick nip from the bottle. Just medicinal, she told herself. Then she rushed up to her room. Grabbing her thick, North Face coat, slipping it on, she poked around, looking for her woolly hat. Content she had dressed warmly, Justyna walked out onto the balcony of her room. The door resisted as she pushed against the settled snow outside, then she tested her footing on the wet surface.

The view was beautiful. Snow had blanketed the entire area. Whichever way she looked, the snow had covered the landscape like a blank canvas. No signs of life, no tire marks, no footsteps, nothing. It was unlike any winter scene she had seen. Yes, it snowed everywhere. Of course, she had seen it before, yet it was always in busy towns or cities, traffic churning the snow to grey slush and people leaving traces of their presence. This was something different. It was just a white sheet, draped across the land. She was desperate to get out and leave her own footprints, like discovering a deserted island where the only footprints in the sand were your own.

She made her way down to the lounge. Unlocking the French doors, she stepped out into the snow. It was not too cold. She still took a hit from the flask, though, the warm spiced rum warming her as it made its way into her stomach. The snow was deeper than she imagined it would be, falling as it had in such a brief time. Then she made her way around the hotel, keeping close to the building. She checked out the outhouses, trying doors and making sure all the doors had been locked.

Justyna passed a little stairway, which led down to an enormous iron door. Snow had covered the first few steps, the rest shrouded in darkness and cobwebs. It seemed to go underground, as there was no building above the stair level. Perhaps an old storage room, Justyna thought. She wasn't a fan of spiders or their webs. She decided it was safer to check it another time.

Soon she was back at where she started. Her footsteps were clear in the snow from when she started out her walk. Justyna lifted her foot, scraping the snow off on the garden wall, clearing a space to sit. Perched on the edge of the cleared spot on the wall, she lit another cigarette and took another sip of her drink. It looked so peaceful as she looked across the garden. From her room, she had seen a path leading through the woods at the rear of the garden. She would see if the path led through the trees to the beach. The snow was now crunching under her feet as the surface of the snow froze. Snow-covered pine trees had kept the snow off the forest floor, creating a little sheltered walkway — like a tunnel — just past the opening in the fence. Justyna stood by the fence, peering into the forest. It looked like a fairy tale scene, as the snow-covered trees had given the forest interior a darker, eerie, silent look down through the track. She walked into the pine forest, following the shadowy, well-worn pathway.

"Lions and tigers and bears, oh my," she said, laughing.

Soon the path opened wider, the trees became sparser, and the sound of crashing waves echoed around her. Wind blew from the sea, chilling her face, as she stepped out of the forest onto the beach, leaving the sheltered path. It was worth it, as the view was amazing. In either direction was just miles of sandy beach. Across the water, she could make out the town of Poole. There were little islands dotted across the bay. Even in this chilly, winter season, the attraction was easy to see. It was clear to Justyna that even in the unpredictable summer months, it would be the perfect place to spend time in. The sand dunes along the beach supplied the ideal spot to shelter from the wind, so Justyna found a nice little clump of sand reeds, and she took a seat on the cold ground. It was a small sacrifice, considering the view along the natural harbour. It was relaxing, even in the cold. Ever since she had worked in the Caribbean, nothing in the UK reminded her of her time in the beautiful locations she was lucky to have worked in. This was as close as it got. It was easy to imagine that on a sunny summer's day, if you added palm trees.

CHAPTER 3

Steve Young-Ballard, or Steve Young, as he preferred, was the last heir to the Young-Ballard Estate. It was a great residence with working dairy farms, forestry district and lucrative fishing rights —an affluence of revenue for the household. Yet Steve shunned this, preferring to distant himself from the family, much to his parents' anxiety. They demanded he accept a commission in the armed services; they needed this of him, like the men of the family had done before him.

Steve was bright. He attended some of the finest schools in the country. He soon learned of the family's history; the links to how his great grandfather, Nathaniel Ballard, indulged in slavery to create their fortunes. Any typical young person would jump at the chance to have such security at a youthful age, being waited on hand and foot. Cars and holidays — appreciating one day that you would be the head of all that richness. Steve, not so much. He had his own ethics about the family history, aware it was an unpleasant one. His mother tried over the years to show it was ancient history. History crowded society with legacies made up from a dark trading past. Even how they treated the employees was in fact looked down upon from the patriarchs in his family. Still, it was not for him. He demanded recognition for who he was, not what he was due to inherit. He wanted people to admire him for who he was, not what he had and who his relatives were.

Steven had sufficient savings from his younger days, to go his own way. He stayed local, living in Poole. He travelled when he wished, travelling to places where people either worked or starved. He came home one day to set up his own men's barbershop. His innate talent at business soon saw him with a chain of successful, established shops across the district. He was popular for both his shops and his personality. He was a well-liked individual, who knew and had a good relationship with all his fellow artists.

This soon altered when his grandma, who he cherished, called him to the estate house at Rempstone. She told him he was going to inherit the estate, anyway; it was up to him to manage the estate as an ongoing business. Aware of how his mind functioned, she perceived that if she told him that the land would go to the National Trust, many people would lose their income, even their houses. Would he decline to acknowledge his commitments? He must come back and work for the family. The estate depended on him taking over. It was a family business.

They talked for hours. He offered his side across, expressing that the entire culture of Nathaniel Ballard was false, that he was a merciless man, and that the family should have no connections to the richness he had set up on the back of suffering and torment. His grandmother warned him, even though the estate now had produced an extensive volume of positive qualities, offering promise to the residents, careers, training fellowships and so much more. If he came back and worked for the family, even in a job of his preference, he could keep the estate to gratify him. She demanded to know that she was leaving behind the estate in excellent hands. As his father had died, he was the heir; he had to step up.

As he drove into the vast lands of Rempstone Manor, memories came flooding back. The track meandered around the edge of the forest, to one side. The other was a sweeping view of a large lake, situated at the bottom of far-stretching fields. He drove up to the front of the house — a three-storey, grey manor. Enormous carved lions sat at the base pillars of the granite steps that led up to two huge oak doors. Two Christmas trees had been placed at either side of the doors, lightly decorated. Steven smiled, as they were the same trees he remembered from his childhood. His gran never wasted or replaced what was not needed to be changed. He was about to bang on the large, black door knockers, when the door was pulled open.

"Ah, Rothman, you're still alive then, waiting on Gran at every beck and call."

Rothman was his gran's confidante and personal butler. He had served his gran for as long as Steven could remember. He was a tall, thick-set man; slightly greying now, yet still looking fit and healthy, even if he was. Steven tried to guess his age. Fifty, he thought.

"You're late, sir, as always. Your gran is waiting for you."

"Of course, that is why she called me back."

Steven made his way through to find his gran, passing from elegant room to room. Finding her, she welcomed him with a gentle hug, and a kiss on the cheek. She poured him a drink and sat down next to him, patting his thigh.

Steven looked over at her, taking her hand and kissing the back of it. Grandma Beryl was a stalwart of the family. Right or wrong, she would stand and uphold the name. She may have used a stick now, to steady herself, yet she was strong, focused and wily. Often getting what she wanted, you crossed her at your peril. She dressed very chic, her hair and makeup always immaculate. She was, even in her twilight years, an attractive lady. She was well spoken, and polite in her mercenary attitude. She did not suffer fools.

"You have been my pride and joy, Steven. Even when you got all uppity and tenacious, you made me proud. Your grandpa would be proud of you, doing what you assumed was proper. You stood your ground and believed in what you said and did."

"Even refusing to follow him into the army. Do you think that would have pleased him to know? I doubt it, Grandma,"

"Oh, he loathed the military. He was like you in more ways than you understand. Why do you think he sold the land? No, he would have been proud of what you have achieved out on your own."

Steve accepted the drink, thanking her as he took in what he was learning.

"Then why did Mother flip out about the whole means? It was as if I had committed a sin."

"Your mother is an old guard. A spoilt upbringing, never had to work. It is all network and culture, tea parties and shopping. She was more concerned she would lose face amongst her jam and Jerusalem friends."

She crossed to the other side of the room, pulling the dangling cord. She returned to sit beside him.

"I may be your loving grandmother, and you will forever be the apple of my eye, however, do not think that I will not cut you from the family wealth, Steven. I know you still collect your allowance every month, so you are not that proud."

"Grandma, say it how you see it then — straight to the point as ever," he said. He leant over to kiss her cheek. "What is it you want me to do? Take over everything? I would not know where to begin. I am no farmer."

"You do not need to be a farmer and take over everything. Just come back, work on the estate here and there, and let the residents see you're part of the family. You are the heir. Give them something to identify with;

you are part of the family anew. If you do not, your name will have no recognition other than someone who has gained all this, just for the wealth. Your good name will be nothing more than, 'young Steven got everything and sold it for his own purpose.'"

"I grew up on the estate. They recognize me. They know me well enough to know that I am better than that."

"You think so — watch."

With that declared, the door opened and the house butler entered the room, bidding Steven's grandma good morning and offering his services. He strutted around the room to confront her, not noticing her visitor, at first.

"Mr Steven, sir, this is an unforeseen comfort. It has been…" The butler searched for the correct phrase, trying not to irritate the guest. "Well, a lengthy time, sir. Is there anything I, or we, can do for you?"

"Rothman, please bring in a round of tea and sandwiches, for us both, please. Steven will have coffee."

"Is the young sir staying then?" Rothman asked.

"For now," she responded, waiting as Rothman left the room.

"However you think you left, they appear not to look at you in the same light. You are just a family member, taking an inheritance each month, giving nothing back."

"That is a mischievous trick to bring me back in the fold, Grandma," he grinned.

"Of course. Like I said, I love you, Steven. I need you to come back to the family. I am well informed of how your outlets are doing — your little empire is most splendid. Now it is time to look after what we have as a family."

"Doing what? I have no background on managing the land. What do you suggest I do? You no doubt have an idea already."

"Of course I do. You will be the estate squire, checking the fishing runs, make sure the fences are intact, make safe our borders. Of course, you will have personnel who will oversee the workers of the estate. Your position will be to make sure they are performing their duties. Nothing too taxing; it is a position your father, his father and so forth, has all worked. Do you agree?"

"Do I have much of a choice?"

"Nothing that I can see." She rose, cupping his face and kissing his forehead.

"What about that house — the hotel? Does it still belong to us — maybe rented or leased?" he asked.

"Nothing to do with the family. That dark side of the family is no longer our burden and no longer your consideration," she answered in a stern voice.

"They haunt it Grandma, it is a wrong place. I used to go there when I was younger, and I heard things."

"That may be true, but the land, along with that house, is no longer our concern. Just try to remember that you are serving the family and me. You have no need to worry about that hotel. I know you will not let me down."

Beryl knew the history of that hotel, and knew extremely well what dark secrets it had. It was passed down to her from her parents. The family, like many others, had a bad side back in the past. Although not all of them held such an evil past. Yes, she knew what he was referring to, about seeing things. It was indeed haunted, even if modern society had not really proven the existence of ghosts, apart from half-hearted shows on TV, or theatres having so-called mediums that conned desperate widows and families into thinking that they could pass messages over to them from their loved ones from the so-called other side. If they wanted to see real spirits, then they should spend some time in The Chine. They would not be so keen to contact the dead after that.

That was how it started. Steven had been back for three years now. He discovered that he appreciated the liberation the position offered him; no more having to stress over his businesses. He stood making idle chit-chat, repeating the same things. This was a far better office to work in. Walking the estate, shotgun in hand, he even adopted a German Shepherd who went along with him on his walks. They grew to be the strongest of friends. Wherever he went, she went too. He called her Gypsy, because she was seeming to belong to the land as much as he now did. She loved the opportunity of running around the woodland and open areas, hiding up in the heather in the summer, waiting for him to catch up. Then she would bound out to startle him before charging off anew. Yet, when he ordered her, she knew to show up and settle by his side. Unless he was at the edge of the forest, next to The Chine, Gypsy sat behind him, showing that something in that building was wrong. Often her hair would go up, her teeth showing as she growled at something that she either saw or sensed. Steve would ruffle her head, telling her not to worry and that they were not passing any further. He would watch, though. Even at night he would wander along the beach, following the track to The Chine. There he would lean against a tree, just watching. Every time he left, he had seen something he knew was not ordinary. It was not a good thing, but rather an evil thing.

Today they were out walking along the shore, heading towards the edge of the estate. The wind was getting up, blowing from the east, bringing with it a thick snowstorm. Gypsy was running in and out of the surf, chasing the waves. Steve was looking up ahead just as Justyna stepped out from the tree line. Gypsy halted in the surf, one leg bent, as if pointing at the intruder. A swift whistle from Steve had her walking beside him, step for step. He saw it was the girl from the hotel. Who else would walk from that path? It was the only one that lead to this part of the beach. He continued to walk towards her, keeping his pace the same. As he came closer, he shouted out to her.

"Good morning! Do not worry; the dog is friendly. You must be the lady looking after The Chine."

Even if he knew she was, it was an effective way to break the ice.

"I am, yes. Dogs are fine — I like dogs."

She bent down, slapping her thighs and calling the dog.

Gypsy looked up at Steve, waiting for permission to leave his side. With a nod of his head, the dog was at Justyna's side, wallowing at the fuss she was making.

"Oh, friendly, great, big, fluffy dog. My name is Justyna. And yes, I am the winter housekeeper, I guess you could say."

Steve removed his glove, offering his hand to her, feeling the cold of hers as she shook his hand.

"You're frozen. Do you want to borrow these?" he asked, taking the other glove off.

"That's very kind. I never expected it to be this cold," she laughed.

"Its fine, take them. I am sort of used to the climate here. How are you finding the place?"

She slipped the gloves on as she answered. She said it was OK, if a little strange, yet also nice to be on her own and have time to think. The warmth of the gloves felt comforting.

"Strange in what way?" he asked, trying to hide his fears of The Chine from her.

The Chine. "It is so big, and it's just me. Maybe I could rent this big, fluffy beast," she joked, stroking Gypsy's head.

They chatted as they walked along the beach, talking about this and that. Steve told her that the snow would fall heavier through the next few days. He also told her that the hotel was safe, and that there was no crime around these parts. Even as the words left him, he knew she was not safe in that place. He knew Martin; he would have made sure she had all she needed, to a small degree.

"So, what do you do? It is very quiet here, almost a silent place. Is there other work here for any locals, other than the hotel?"

Over the next twenty minutes, Steve explained who he was and why he was there. She listened with interest, offering him a cigarette. As they walked back up the path, through the trees, to The Chine, they chatted more, as if they were old friends. She liked him — he seemed very relaxed and honest. Of course, he was attractive. He had friendly eyes, she thought. She was not so sure about the beard. It was not a full, huge beard, just small and neatly trimmed. She wondered what he looked like without it, since she had no way to compare if it suited him or not. Still, she was glad they had met. He would keep her company from time to time, or just pop in for a coffee.

They reached the gate to the grounds of The Chine.

"This as far as we go, Justyna. We have to head off along the track, check on the deer and make sure they have enough food on the ground," he told her.

"Here, you better take your gloves back."

"No, its fine, hang onto them. I can get them later."

"Ah, later; as in when you come knocking on the door late at night," she mocked him.

"I am not that sort of guy. How dare you, madam," he replied in the same tone.

"Well, please do. You're welcome to come for a drink anytime."

"Yes. Here, take this. Call me anytime if you need anything."

He took a card from his wallet and offered it to her. She slipped it inside her glove. Steve dropped his cigarette butt on the floor, wishing her well as he turned to walk away. Justyna bent down to stroke Gypsy and say goodbye to her new friend. The exposed teeth shocked her, and she pulled her hand away. Gypsy was looking ahead, past her, backing away from the garden gate.

"Oh, my god, is she OK?" she asked, worried.

"Ah, she may have caught the scent of a fox, or seen a rabbit she wants to chase after. Gypsy has been well trained. So she will not chase anything unless I say so," he lied.

"Ah, bless her. Well, ok. Tomorrow I will bring coffee, and we can meet again at the beach."

"If you add brandy, you are on. Coffee on its own — you will be lucky if it is just the dog."

"Brandy, eh. Well, you are just my kind of man, Steve."

Her face blushed at the comment, realizing she sounded too keen.

They both seemed lost for words, so they hugged and made their way in separate directions, bidding farewell. Justyna cursed herself for revealing such an awkward confession.

Steve smiled at the fact that she gave her attraction away so fast, although he seemed happy with the comment. He thought she was attractive. Even though he could only see her face, he knew she had the full figure he liked. Her eyes were friendly, and she seemed very genuine.

Steve turned, tracking back to the edge of the trees, looking into the hotel gardens. Gypsy started to whine, as if distressed. Of course she would react like that — they both knew what evil was in that hotel. So he reached down to her, stroking her head and comforting her, as they both looked across the garden as Justyna made her way round to the lounge doors, disappearing inside. Steve looked up at the third floor, the turret room to the right of the hotel. Snow soon fell again; thicker, as he had predicted. The wind was now picking up, swirling the snow up and over the already snow-laden hedges. The shadow moved across the window to the next window in the turret. Its face was hard to make out from so far away, but it was a face, and it was looking back at him. Gypsy barked, her fur raised and her teeth bared in her anger. Steve turned back towards the trees, calling his companion to follow. This was a dilemma, as he knew he would have to go in The Chine for a drink now. The spirits knew, and the ghosts of his past knew, that he was coming.

Steve looked down at Gypsy walking beside him. "You, my girl, you stay at home."

Justyna walked back into the hotel, happy that she bumped into the young Steve. She cursed herself for sounding so keen. After what the last few months had thrown at her, falling so quick for another man was not the way she planned her life to go. However, she could not help feeling he was genuine. He was tall as well, plus he seemed in perfect health, as well as fit. Justyna had had a sneaky look at his ass, but with all the winter clothing, it was too hard to tell. Hopefully he would turn up for a drink.

As she made her way to the bar, she could hear Gypsy barking. Not once did she consider it was because of The Chine's hidden secrets, nor did she put it down to the dog being really frightened to enter the hotel gardens. Such was her oblivious excitement at meeting her new friend.

Upstairs in the tower room, the lights flickered into life, on and off. The furniture shook, and the room grew icy cold. Shadows grew from the walls, stretching out across the room, like fingers reaching out and searching. The shadows halted at the base of the large balcony window, forming upwards into a black mass, taking the shape of a human shadow. The blackness turned grey, as the image of a grim-faced man stared out across the rear of the hotel. Rage filled the room, accumulating into a deep, echoing roar, as the figure watched the bearded man walk away through the trees.

Justyna turned the volume up on the speakers in the bar, as she poured herself a glass of red wine, singing along to the current song. The roar of anger from the upstairs room was disguised by her singing. She turned to lower the volume on the speakers, thinking she heard something — someone shouting. She walked back to the lounge, going to the French windows and checking, hoping to see that Steve had changed his mind about the coffee.

After seeing nothing, she turned to go back to her room. "Calm down, silly, you're acting like a schoolgirl," she told herself.

After Justyna collected the bottle from the bar, she thought she would have a nice jacuzzi before she settled in for the rest of the day. An hour later, up to her neck in foam bubbles, Justyna sank back in the large jacuzzi bath. Her bottle of wine was beside her within easy reach, the half-full glass in her hand. Perfect — the bath felt amazing. She felt hot and relaxed, with an excellent red wine. She played with the switches, sending hot jets across the lower half of her hidden body. Air jets played with her senses, making her giggle. Hot water mixed with the wine soon had her relaxed, feeling happy for the first time in weeks. It was easy to look back now at how she had gotten herself into such a mess. Pushing the thoughts away, Justyna closed her eyes, enjoying the relaxing warmth of the bath. She tried to forget about all the shouting and arguing that she had gone through.

Not being a person who liked confrontation, it had taken a lot of courage for her to stand up to Julian, her partner. They had been together for too long to call him a boyfriend. All that wasted time, thinking she knew him. She had trusted him. Not once did she think he was cheating on her. Oh, of course her friends all knew. They soon brought names to light the minute she left him. Try as she may, she could not keep the bad thoughts out of her head, remembering the last row — how he had screamed at her, grabbing her arms and shaking her. Each action was fresh in her mind, as she pictured him pulling his arm back, his hand swinging down towards her face. Even now it felt so real.

In fact, it was real. Justyna was not sure if she felt the blow first or heard the impact of the slap across the side of her face first. She struggled to keep her composure in the warm water, sliding under the bubbles. The impact of the blow across her cheek made her drop her wineglass. Her eyes opened wide as the shock swept over her, her face stinging. She was not sure if it was the wine mixed with the heat from the bath, and if that was why it felt so real.

Sitting up, one hand held the side of the bath, and the other searched in the water for her glass. Looking around the room, she felt on edge. She rose out of the bath, taking her time, still not sure what was going on, and she placed the glass on the side. She raised her hand to her face. It was stinging. Was the strike her imagination, or was it real? Was it the wine, or the heat of the bath?

Looking into the mirror over the hand basin, Justyna wiped away the condensation from the glass, staring at herself, confused at what had just happened. Marks of a finger were visible on her face. As she gently stroked her cheek, she could feel the heat from the contact. Not sure what to do, she tried in vain to make sense of what was going on. A single tear crept down across her tingling cheek. She panicked, rushing across to the bathroom door and slamming it shut. She locked it and leant against the door. Then she sank down to the floor, keeping her back pressed to the door. Was someone in the room? If so, who, and how did they get in? Why would they slap her across the face? She raised herself up to take the robe from the back of the door, covering herself up. It was strange — she felt naked now, tying the cord around her waist. Of course there was nobody in the room. It had to be the heat and the wine. She was tired; the past few days had been hectic. Her imagination was on overload. Yes, that was it. She unlocked the door, pulled it open and marched into the room.

"See? For fuck's sake, get hold of yourself, Justyna, or it is going to be a nightmare here," she said out loud.

Now sat on the bed, she began to compose herself once more. She dried her hair as she watched herself in the wardrobe mirrors. Turning her head to the side, she noticed that the red welts of the impact were still visible. Briefly she tried looking for an explanation, her mind trying to justify her excuses for the incident. Perhaps it had been such a turning point in her life, that she had relived it to remind herself never to get in a situation like that again — a semi-conscious warning. But it was real, as if she were recalling every second of the moment again. But why? She was over it.

Placing her palm across the slapped cheek, all she could feel now was the warmth of her own hand. Justyna made her way back to the bathroom, first peering inside before stepping in. She emptied the tub, collecting the wine bottle from the side. Had she drunk the entire bottle? It was possible. That, and the hot bath. Yes, that was what it was. On an empty stomach. Too much, even for her, she thought, as she began dressing again.

Justyna paused for a while, just to listen. There was a tiny amount of doubt in her mind as to her own explanation of the event. Dressed, she made her way downstairs to the lounge, stopping on the stairs, touching her cheek again, not knowing why she did so.

Again she listened, just for a second, peering down the staircase, bending at the knees, looking into the hallway.

Was she looking for something that she never believed in, knowing nothing was there? Now she felt angry with herself. Not with the incident, but for letting James once again ruin her day. It was just stupid, acting this way. James had always made her doubt herself. Even now, although they were no longer an item, he was still getting inside her head. Justyna swore to herself that this would be the last time he ever did that.

Ghosts don't hit people, she thought to herself.

At the back of her mind, deeply hidden where you shut things away, forcing them out of all consciousness, she knew she was not alone. Soon she would know this, but for now, her stubborn belief that it was just her imagination, was enough.

All her beliefs that ghosts did not exist, would soon be proved wrong. What was about to happen for Justyna would not just change her beliefs, but her whole future.

CHAPTER 4

Beryl Ballard-Young was born to be a lady of the manor. With the best schooling, she was groomed to marry into money. Her own parents were Lord and Lady Hougan. They owned a vast amount of land in the Lake District. They were also very influential in the government of their time. Lord Hougan was a civil engineering stalwart, who had helped develop a great deal of London's underground network structures.

Beryl Ballard had not spent too much time at the family home, being bordered at schools across the country for most of her school life. So, for her, family life was particularly important, as she never felt she had that connection with her parents. As soon as she was married, she swore that when she had children of her own, they would be a close part of the family, not packed away to school for much of their young life.

With this in place, she became the matriarch of the family. What she said, went. Even when she became a grandparent, her domination over the family stood strong. Of course, Lord Ballard had his say in the family affairs, but it was clear to the family that Lord Ballard ran his businesses with a rod of iron, and Lady Ballard was the head of the family. You did things her way, or you did nothing.

She was not stuck up or pompous, nor did she just socialize with the landowners, or rich well-to-do types, unless it was needed for protocol. She was an avid supporter of challenging work. If you were good at your job and knew how to hold an intelligent conversation, you were as good as anyone. Hence why she saw no reason for her daughter, Annabelle, not to marry a commoner, as it was said.

Annabelle Ballard, the one and only child, married a young, navy officer, Ethan Young. He came from an ordinary, working-class family from Bristol. He went to university to study media, only to feel that it was not physical enough for him. He wanted to travel and find some excitement. As soon as he had his degree, he took a commission in the Royal Navy. He reached the rank of captain and could have gone on to a much higher rank. That was until he met Anabelle. It was love at first sight, so he resigned his commission and took a role on the estate; of course, under the suggestion of Beryl. He passed away from a severe heart attack in his early fifties. Steve was devastated, as he and his father were close. His mother, Anabelle, not so much. They were simply different people. They loved each other very much, but Anabelle was more about the title, being the daughter of the Ballard family, and a major landowner in the region. The need to play the lady of the manor type of role, she saw as a duty rather than a chore. She loved being on the more exclusive boards. Her influence gave her a little bit of power, which was more than she received at home. As Beryl put it, she belonged to the Jam and Jerusalem set.

Beryl Ballard was in her early seventies now; she needed a stick to walk, at times. Yet she was as bright today as she ever was. But now, time was running out for her. Her grandson had to step up to the mark —take over what was theirs by right. She knew he was happy where he was. But it was time to come home — stop being so headstrong and join the family. She loved him dearly and admired what he had achieved on his own. The monthly allowances were always paid out to him. So he was not against taking the family money.

She was a tall lady — six feet — and still extremely attractive. Her makeup was expertly done. Anabelle, being a follower of fashion, had shown her the best tones for her skin and how to apply it to her best advantage. Anabelle may not have been the most qualified in the family, but she knew all there was to know about fashion and beauty.

Beryl had a full, even figure, and she looked years younger. She put it all down to fresh air and good, old-fashioned, demanding work.

'Never ask someone to do a job you would not do yourself.' That was Steven's dad's motto, one that Beryl had followed along.

Beryl now stood in the main lounge of the house, looking out across the open driveway and beyond into the fields. Lost in her thoughts, she never heard Rothman enter with her morning coffee. He stood watching her, knowing she was worried about something.

"Is everything OK, my lady? You only stare out of the window when you have something on your mind," he said.

She turned, laughing at the suggestion. He passed her the coffee, watching her as she took her usual seat beside the fireplace.

"You know me so well. Do I have other tell-tale signs that you know of, Edgar?"

"Enough to know you would never beat me at poker," he replied.

"It is young Steven; I know he is right about this damn hotel. I heard that he was meeting the young housekeeper they have looking after it. We should have demolished when we had the chance."

"Yes, I did hear that they were seen talking on the shore, but it was just one meeting. I doubt it will come to much more."

"Though it is not that, you know what it is, Edgar. It is that bloody house, or hotel. Call it what you will."

"Does he know the whole story of the house, or just that he does not like it? I recall him saying, back in his younger days, that it had ghosts in it; that he thought it was haunted."

"No, he thinks just as you confirmed. Haunted, but he is inquisitive. He has no idea what evil lay behind those walls. It was enough for him to condemn the family for the slavery links his ancestors made our fortunes from. This, I fear, would bring the family down completely."

"Will you tell him or wait to see how things play out? Perhaps discourage him from pursuing such a relationship, if you feel that is where he is going."

"He is my grandson; he is so much like me. Should I try that, it will push him more toward her," she laughed.

Beryl drank her coffee, sitting back to relax, trying to figure out the best way to inform her grandson of the true horror of The Chine —what it was that was so evil, lurking behind the closed doors of the hotel.

"Do you think the young girl will be in trouble? Or even Steven?" Rothman asked.
"The girl, yes, perhaps scared. I do not think she will be in any real danger. How they managed to get her to stay there is a mystery. How they even manage to keep the godforsaken hotel open at all is a bigger one," Beryl added.

"I can help with this one. I bumped into Martyn Cupps in the village the other day. They told her it was just closed for the festive period, due to the severe weather forecasted. And they needed a temporary caretaker. She was promised a full-time job in the new season," Rothman replied. "She was professionally qualified as a manager herself, with a very impressive CV. He wanted to tell her about the hotel — the strange goings-on, as he put it. But that Greensmith chap hushed him up; told him to say nothing. And worse, they just gave her a quick tour then left her there on her own, within hours of her arriving,"

"Poor girl. Well, if she just keeps herself sane, then she will have nothing to worry about. If Steven gets involved with this girl — if he goes into the hotel — who knows how he will react," Beryl said.

She walked back to the window, her cup in hand. Her beverage now tasted sour.

"When I say, 'how he will react', you know who I mean, don't you, Edgar?"

"Yes, I do. You mean Nathanial."

They left the conversation there. It was pointless discussing it further, as they both knew trouble was coming. Not knowing how the ancient ghost — a tortured ghost, one who in his own right being the forebear of the family ancestry —would react to a modern heir entering his domain, was not something either wanted to dwell on. Especially since the family had mentally pushed him to insanity, resulting in him taking his own life.

Beryl walked across the hall to the family library, closing the doors behind her. She took a seat at the large, elegant, regency Chas Norman writing desk. She poured herself a brandy from the decanter set, placed on the corner of the desk. Then she took out a large, old-style book from the drawer. The book was a ship's log, bound in leather with small, braided ties bound together to keep it sealed.

The first pages showed the name of the ship, the *Lady Prudence*. A three-mast galleon that had been captured from the Portuguese some years earlier. Now the *Lady Prudence* was a formidable, armed, cargo carrier, with a well-paid, trained and experienced crew. The log told where it was sailing from, and to where its destination would be; who was commanding the ship, along with the dates. This continued throughout each journey, detailed through the entire log. Beryl skipped ahead a little, finding a sailing from Portsmouth to the West Indies in the summer of 1850. It was Nathaniel Ballard's last trade journey to the Caribbean.

Nathaniel's idea was to follow the triangular trade routes, which took the so-called British traders to exchange goods from the homeland. In fact, it was mostly a fake trade route, which, before the abolition of slavery, took them to collect slaves from the many overflowing factories scattered along the islands, hiding under the guise of trading fruits, molasses and sugar. Slaves from west Africa, young families included, were sold, often forced to separate from each other.

Thousands died en route at the hands of heartless slavers, who were told that if the slaves were too weak or slowed the harsh trek through the hot and dry routes, they were to be left behind to die. Nathaniel Ballard was no fool. He was aware of the situation, yet he chose to ignore the realities of slavery, in order to further his own

89

plantations growth without the cost of an expanding workforce. So he began paying the black workers a meagre wage. Then he charged them for living on the plantations, thus gaining his money back.

This time, his journey was to add to his home estates workers. He was looking for reliable, presentable staff for the Ballard estate back in Dorset — slaves under the guise of working household staff. He had been given land along the south coast, where he had built a vast estate with a beautiful house. Leandro, his friend and confident captain of the *Prudence*, had heard from various other traders that the Haitians were formidable workers, abandoned by the slavers because of the uprisings against them. Leandro had heard these young slaves were in better health, as their journey to the factories were short, not having been forced to journey long distances, as were the African slaves.

This was not the case by a long way, as the treatment of the Haitians was atrocious. They were treated so severely that most slaves died by the age of twenty-one. Eventually this led to the island revolting, with the support of the French, who supplied military generals to turn on their captors, forcing them to flee the island. An interception, which at the time was ideal, later proved costly to the island, where they would be paying back debts for generations to come.

For Nathaniel this was irrelevant, as he had the pick of the last of the few remaining slaves from the island. Unrest was strong, as word had got back to the slaves that their homeland was free. Their desire to return home was now stronger than ever. But any suggestion of revolt was beaten back out of them, and the slavers took any rumblings of dissent out on the young and old.

Leandro set sail back to the homeland, with a cargo of fruits, sugars and various other goods. Below the decks of the galleon, in the lowest holds, were the slaves. They had more space than most slaves were given, as there were only eight of them: five males aged between fourteen and twenty-six years, and three women — one in her late teens, another just twenty, and one much older. All sat huddled against the wall of the hold, whispering to each other, only to fall silent at the sign of any approaching crew member. They would only stare at their captors.

It was noted that the younger of the boys had made a sort of figurine out of bone and hair. He was always twisting the hair around the bone, until it began to envelope the bone completely. Younger guards were made to feel uneasy, complaining to the crew that the Haitians were voodoo worshipers. It was a myth soon put to rest by Leandro, who threatened to flog anyone mentioning voodoo aboard the ship again. He would also throw the slaves overboard, angering their gods, a fear far worse than any locked-up voodoo slave could inflict. It was never mentioned again.

Beryl read on, as the logbook showed the journey all the way back to Poole harbour. It mentioned nothing further of real interest —a few ailments dealt with by the ship's doctors, tooth extractions, and stitching of minor wounds. There was no mention of any discipline handed out to the crew, showing that the ship was well-captained by Leandro. Wages were logged down on the date the ship docked. No further logs were added after — this was the last recorded voyage of the *Lady Prudence*. Beryl noticed that the records showed no mention of the slaves being loaded or unloaded. Just the other contents were logged.

For Nathaniel Ballard, bringing those few slaves home would be the biggest mistake of his life. Worse even, as it would lead to the end of his life, along with two of his closest, beloved friends. It was obvious that as soon as the cargo was unloaded and sent off to various distributors, under cover of darkness the slaves were taken ashore at Studland Bay, where they were swiftly taken to the manor house, The Chine. A long way from home, afraid and cold, the slaves made their way along the wooden dock, each holding onto the shoulder of the person in front, looking all around them. They tried to take in the unfamiliar sights that greeted them — the noises and the voices all alien to them. The only sure thing they knew was that they were a long way from home, and they would never be going back.

CHAPTER 5

Beryl closed the book then drained her glass, pouring another. She felt cold suddenly, just from the thought of the history that followed the last voyage of her distant grandfather. It was well known within the family, passed down in tales from parent to parent. Large oil paintings adorned the walls of the new manor house. Each had history attached to their names. Not all were good and true men though, as each family throughout the world has a history. The Ballard family history did have some very influential members, ones who had made an historic mark on the changing society throughout the centuries, though little was said or recorded of the dark side that Nathaniel Ballard had brought to their land. Beryl knew — she wished she never, as it was a not a good family story.

She walked across to the window, looking across the rear of the landscaped gardens, where the distant woodland formed a barrier between the estate and The Chine. It was a fair distance — a mile or more — The Chine hidden away on the far side of the forest. Still not far enough for her. Beryl pulled the cord, closing the large velvet drapes and shutting the late afternoon sun out, her desk lamp now supplying the room's only light.

It threw out a circle of light around the desk, as if a large spotlight were hanging from the ceiling. Beryl skirted around the desk, walking across to the fireplace where she placed her drink atop the large mantle. She pulled on the bell cord then took her drink back to the desk, where she sat waiting for Rothman.

After a few minutes the door was opened, and the light from the hallway mimicked the doorframe. Rothman's shadow stretched into the room as he stepped across the threshold, his shadow shrinking.

"Yes, my lady, can I help?"

"Edgar, the fire. I think I feel a chill coming."

"Of course. The room will be warm in no time."

He bent down in front of the fire and busied himself. Within seconds the fire flickered into life. Logs and kindling crackled and splintered as they caught. Rothman stood, waiting for the fire to catch all over. When it had, he placed a few larger logs on. The smell of pine filled the room as the logs began to burn.

"There we go. Are you sure you would not feel warmer in the summer house, or even the family room? This room always feels cold."

Beryl shook her head, saying she was fine where she was. "I am not surprised it is cold in here. A lot of the family history, good and bad, has been stored here on these shelfs. Our bloodline often ran cold and unpleasant, Edgar."

"Well, if you need me, I am close by."

With that, he left her looking through the bookshelves, trying to find a certain unmarked, untitled book. It was where it always was, tucked away behind the second volume of the West Indies shipping routes. It was a leatherbound, unmarked book — more of a diary than a book. It held a mixture of entries from Nathaniel Ballard — his plans for his workforce of slaves and how he saw the influence of the estate profiting the region. As the entries went on, it was clear to see that the man had begun to lose his mind. His entries became unclear — he suspected that the slaves were bewitching the estate.

Beryl took a seat beside the fire, placing the book on the small table. The warmth of the room was now to her liking, as the glow of the fire began dancing around the bookshelf and walls at the far side of the room. She had read the book repeatedly throughout her years, never really understanding the true reasoning behind it all. Was Nathaniel always a cruel man deep inside? It seemed not, judging from the ship's logs. His crew seemed more than happy. The same names seemed to crop up each time a new voyage was planned. There was never any mention of severe actions taken against the crew while they sailed. Even his love-interest was an influential, admirable lady of the time. Yet as the diary explained, something had changed in him to make him act in such a way.

Beryl had spent more time than she needed trying to justify the actions of Nathaniel. She tried to figure out where it all went wrong for him, convinced it was to do with the last voyage he made. The story of voodoo had a part in his downfall.

She sat back, remembering the days of her youth, playing on the estate where she mixed with the children of the workers on the estate. Stories of the haunted, old manor were rife back then. Beryl knew better than most, although she never had to live there. Her seniors had often told ghost stories about the old manor, and the mad Nathaniel who haunted it. Victorians were intrigued and fascinated by the occult, often throwing dinner parties, where the evening entertainment involved Ouija boards and ghost hunts. Of course, it was a much smaller house back then, compared to the manor estate houses of today.

Chine Manor was built with a large stable, and various outhouses filled the courtyard. Even then it gave the estate a grand look. When her father informed the family of the sale of the old manor house, she remembered feeling elated. The house was creepy, and she had seen things — people, dark images looking out of the widows — when the house should have been empty. She had heard the shouting — strange languages crying out. Beryl promised herself that she would never enter the house, having read about Nathaniel's atrocities, a promise she still held to this date.

Beryl emptied her glass, feeling the liquid warm her insides as it made its way through her system. Yet, the goosebumps still enveloped her arms, as the cold overtook the warmth instantly. Beryl looked around the room, searching the shadows. The fire glow cast elongated shapes across the dimly lit room. With each burst of flame, the reflected shadows reached higher to the ceiling, as if they were trying to entomb the room. Slowly, Beryl opened the book. There was no introduction and no forwarding remarks. The book went straight into the family's sworn agreement that the history of Nathaniel Ballard was never to be made known to the public. Only the patriarch of the living family was to know of the history. They were then to ensure the land was never sold; The Chine manor was to be long-term leased for however long it was thought to be seen fit to do so. All the surrounding gardens and The Chine estate was to remain the property of the Ballard estate. Beryl had read the opening page so many times, she could repeat it by sheer memory.

As she read the opening chapter once again, the book revealed how Nathaniel returned from his last voyage with the Haitian slaves. All the slaves were then put to work in The Chine. Two women, Rosaline and Judeline, were to work in the kitchen, with the younger girl, Lovelie, to function as a servant for Nathaniel's fiancé, Annabelle. She would instruct the young girl how to dress her and set out her clothes. She would deal with her needs, as any young servant of the day would do. The idea was that having a black house cleaner would be a huge talking point for the house guests at dinner parties. Annabelle was something of a fashion

97

icon of the day, having recommended the young Queen Victoria on the latest designs currently worn by the gentry of Europe.

Hailing from Paris, Annabelle had worked for the best fashion houses of the day, mixing with the rich and famous at lavish parties. It was here that Anabelle was introduced to the dashing, young Nathaniel, at a royal banquet. She was smitten from the very start, listening to his tales of sailing the West Indies, where he saw and sketched the beautiful colourful outfits of the island women. Nobody had seen such vibrant outfits in the western world, as the dark Victorian dressmakers lacked such boldness. Annabelle wanted to learn and see for herself, having heard how captivating the women looked. From then on, the two became close friends, keeping their romance away from the eyes of court. Only at the secluded Chine estate would they openly express their feelings for each other.

The younger male slaves, Evens and Ricardo, being fit, young slaves, were put to work in the garden with Petersen, the oldest male given a job in the stables. He was taught how to attend the horses, grooming them, mucking out the stables, or weeding and basic garden duties. Other estate workers seemed indifferent to the colour of their understudy's skin. They found them entertaining, listening to them sing or talk to each other in their strange accent. Only the youngest boy, fourteen-year-old Emanuel, caused concern. His companion, although a year older, named Junior, always let the younger boy eat or drink first, as if he had senior authority over him. The book explained how the elder slaves seemed to hold him in awe, as if afraid of him. At the end of the first chapter, the book told how Nathaniel had tried to chastise the boy, making him cry, so the other slaves would see he was just that — a little boy. He held up a horse whip, shouting and waving the whip at the boy, threatening him. Emanuel just stood looking Nathaniel in the eye, as if he was looking through him, not at him. Nathaniel wrote that he had decided to not feed any of the slaves that evening, blaming the lack of gratitude of the young child as the cause for the starvation.

In the following chapter, Nathaniel had written how his own staff had seen the slaves hiding food to make sure the boy had food to eat, should the episode repeat itself. This enraged Nathaniel, as he felt that the slaves had acted in the complete opposite way he had hoped for. All the slaves spoke a little western English, along with a little French.

Beryl read over the section about the senior kitchen girl who had been seen to take bones from the kitchen, hiding them in her apron —this time on the advice of Annabelle, who seemed as nice a woman as Nathanial had described.

Nathaniel had written how he tried to connect with Emanuel. He learnt that the boy spoke a particularly satisfactory level of English, but he had to push him to converse more freely. Nathanial Ballard wrote that the boy seemed shy, but he could not help thinking that the boy was hiding something. The staff often reported that he was always whispering to the other slaves, as if ordering them. His staff also showed concern that the others never made conversation with the boy, unless the boy instigated it. Nathaniel Ballard wrote his concern of what the boy might be; royalty, or at least a tribal chief's son. It concerned him that the love of his life wanted to help the boy. Had he some hold over Anabelle? He wrote of his concerns, how no matter how hard he tried to connect to the boy, he ended up punishing him, only for Anabelle to tell him that he was being too strict.

Beryl, after reading this for the first time, had researched the Haitian tribal groups, searching for something that may explain her ancestor's concerns and his downfall —even just an explanation to the strange occurrences at The Chine. Beryl found out that a lot of the enslaved Africans were mostly Christianized into the Catholic church. They were in fact a mixed group of Dahomean Kongo and Yoruba descendants — a mixed group of West African Vodun. They held the belief that God does not interact with daily life, but that spirits do. Voodoo priests believe in two worlds running side by side — a visible and invisible world. In between the two, they believe the Lwa walk freely. Voodoo priests search out these Lwa, asking for guidance. Beryl discovered that voodoo is not black magic, nor is it considered any less haunting than the Catholic church. It was only feared because it was a slave-based religion, new to the world and dismissed as a false belief. Voodoo curses were all in the mind. This gave Beryl a problem. She knew The Chine was an evil, having earlier thought it was down to the death of the slaves, but she now knew it was something more. Beryl knew she had to seek advice from elsewhere. What Nathaniel did was evil, this Beryl knew. Why he did it, well, that was voodoo. She knew who to call. Only one person could help her.

Beryl poured another drink, before she called for Rothman. He was instructed to call Father Liam and invite him for dinner in two days' time. The invite was expected to be met with compliance. Father Liam was not to be late, and he was to bring the parish registers.

Rothman never needed to ask which registers Father Liam needed to collect and bring. If anyone knew what records Beryl Ballard meant, Father Liam did. Ever since they were children, they had been close friends. Both had played in The Chines grounds; both had seen things that they should never have seen. Yet the truth was there, and now was the time for it to be discovered.

Over the years, although Liam had found a life in the church, the two had been friends. Nothing romantic — simply good old school friends. Beryl, with her family's wealth and contacts, had enough friends in the church. She had been informed of Father Liam's service to the church, and how he had risen to a high level, which had not surprised her. He too, had played in the grounds of The Chine as a child, and as every local child knew, The Chine was not a place to dwell around too long, aside from the normal childhood dare to look inside, or even enter. Liam knew back then that the place was evil. Beryl often wondered if it was this that had helped him find his calling into the dark, demonic investigation side of the church, although back then, he had sworn he would never step foot in that building. Beryl had agreed then, without offering any resistance, as she never had any intention of doing so either.

Now, though, times had changed. Something was wrong. Beryl could feel the rage building, even from the safety of her own surrounds. It was time to confront the dark side of The Chine. Well, Father Liam would.

Enough for today, Beryl thought to herself. Tomorrow she would look further into The Chine story. She had missed a clue, which would explain Nathaniel's demise. For now, she needed to sleep and gather her strength.

Justyna woke early, having not slept too well. She had been waking up throughout the night. Unsure why she was so restless, she drifted in and out of sleep, waking angrier each time, as she tossed and turned, trying to get back to her last dream.

By seven, she had had enough, so she got up to make herself a cup of tea. Tea made, she slipped her robe on and looked out into the garden. Snow had covered the whole grounds. Although it had stopped, it had left a perfect white blanket, with the prevailing winds clearing away any loose debris. The snow formed large drifts against the far end of the landscaped garden. Justyna felt the warm tea invade her body, relaxing her, as she leant against the wooden doorframe.

Then out of the corner of her eye, she saw a movement, fast and instant. Justyna pressed her head against the glass, feeling the cold on her cheek, as she tried to gain a better view over the balcony. She unlocked the door, sliding it open, using her back to push it wider, the icy grip of the snow holding the metal tight. Door open, she gingerly stepped onto the balcony, instantly recoiling her foot, as the cold, frozen floor chilled her bare skin. As she put her slippers on, she ventured out again, both hands cupping her tea. The heat of the tea warmed the China cup, which in turn warmed her.

Justyna looked along the edge of the hotel, searching for the figure. Nothing. It must have been a rabbit or something. Then the laughing began — a child laughter — from the other side of the hotel. Her cup placed on the floor, Justyna wiped the layer of snow off the railing, leaning across it to look the other way. There again, just out of eyeshot, yet enough to know somebody was there. That was when she gazed down to the locked underground cellar she had seen previously. Was that someone standing on the steps, backing away into the shadow and slowly walking backwards down the steps, fading into the darkness? The eyes were just visible. Then it hit her. It was not a shadow dashing in and out of the corner of her eye — it was a child;, a black child.

Justyna wanted to shout out, the brightness of the fresh snow causing her to squint. It was not the surprise of what she thought she saw that stopped her voice from breaking the silence. It was the thunderous roar from inside the hotel —an eerie echoing anger of a roar. She turned so fast she almost lost her footing, causing her to stumble back into her room. The balcony door slammed behind her, as the room turned icy cold. Her cold breath was clearly visible with each exhale she made. She lay where she fell, making no effort to get up. Doors began to slam throughout the hotel, and her own door began to rattle on its hinges.

As the vibrations ended, the crying began — faint crying — but it was clearly crying. Justyna turned her head slightly, as she tried to figure out what was going on. With one hand on the armchair by the balcony door, she pulled herself upright and took a step towards the door. Placing one hand on the doorknob, she turned the key and pulled the door open. She was greeted by distant music being played from the hotel speakers on the lower floors. Slowly she peered out into the corridor, looking one way then the next. Still nothing.

"What the fuck is going on? Was that the wind?" she said out loud. She slammed the door shut again, locking it once more. "Who am I talking to?" she laughed.

It was a nervous laugh; she was not so stupid to know that that was not the wind. She also knew an angry shout when she heard it, having been living with an angry ass of a boyfriend. No, this was something different — strange different. Yet she still never thought that she was in any way in danger. She dismissed any thought of danger, as she wanted to find that child in the garden.

Justyna was soon washed, dressed and walking towards the reception. As she reached the lobby, she stared up at the three portraits, who looked as menacing as they ever did.

"Right, boys, faces to the wall for you, I think. I do not need you watching me every day."

There were a lot of tables to choose from in the lobby that she could stand on to reach the portraits. So she dragged one of the wooden tables across to the wall beneath the portraits, lifting them off their hooks to turn them around. They were heavier than she imagined, and wider. It was a little bit of a struggle. She almost dropped Leandro 's portrait, but she managed to turn them all around. Now they were all propped up against the wall. As she replaced the table, she stood back to admire the work.

"Ah, you all look far better now," she said.

She quickly popped into the reception. Inserting a pod into the Tassimo, she made a fresh coffee, then grabbed a coat from the stand and headed out into the garden. As she rounded the reception desk, the same aroma of lavender descended on her. It was the same scent from the restaurant, the same familiar smell. Once again, she scanned the skirting, searching for a plug-in freshener. It was then that it hit her: the music — the music was playing. She had turned it off the night before, that she was positive about. Justyna stood there in the lobby, looking at the reception desk, wondering how the tape had turned itself on, or if it even did. Confused, she walked back into the rear office of the reception. She pressed 'stop' on the CD player, leaning back to her side towards the reception desk, to make sure it had ceased to play. It had, so she pressed play again, repeating the process over and over. There was no explanation for it. For now it would have to wait, as the child in the garden was more concerning to her. So she walked out of the office and took her coffee from the desk, ready to go and investigate what was going on outside.

As Justyna rounded the desk, she froze. Staring back at her from his portrait against the wall was Nathaniel Ballard —the portrait she had turned just twenty minutes ago. His gaze was solid, as was hers, as Justyna stared into his painted eyes, unmoving. Her mind was blank — not one thought of how, or any offer of an explanation. This time she knew she was right, as he was the first portrait she turned. This time she really felt that he was looking at her. There was no need to move around the lobby to see if his gaze was following her. He was there, staring at her, almost squinting, as if he were trying to make her out and take every detail in. She snapped out of it, breaking the stare and turning around to investigate the hallway.

"Right, who is it? Who is taking the piss? Come on, show yourself. This is not funny at all."

She waited, half knowing there would be no reply. She almost believed that she may have made a mistake, and that she did leave him that way. But again, she knew she did, as he was the main reason for taking the bloody portraits down. This time she would make sure he was looking away. So she turned him round once more, pulled a heavy wingback armchair against the frame, pressing him against the wall. She added a side table to the chair, for extra weight — just to be sure. With a shudder, more nerves than cold, this time, she went outside to look for the child.

CHAPTER 6

Steven had been watching the hotel from his normal, covered position, Gypsy at his side as ever. She was alert, head cocked to one side, trying to find the strange sounds coming from the grounds. Gypsy stepped back, standing behind him. An invisible threat triggered her, causing her follicles to stand on end. Steve dropped his hand, stroking her head and reassuring her.

"I know, girl, I hear it."

Gypsy whined, brave as she was. This was something that even she assumed was wrong for them both. The sudden uproar from the hotel, although not heard for the first time, shocked Steven, loud as it was. Gypsy stepped back a little further. He knelt beside her, his arm around her neck. She licked the side of his face as she barked at him, warning him, as she looked back down the trail, that it was time to leave.

"It's OK, just wait. We have to see if she is safe, girl. Ten minutes more, I promise."

Then he saw the doors on the balcony open and Justyna stepped out. He stood up, then stepped back into the tree line, watching her through the snow-topped trees. Kneeling again to get a better view, he watched her as she leant over the barrier. He wondered what she was doing. She seemed to look at something. Steven searched the open ground in front of him, seeing nothing. Justyna was now leaning right out from the balcony, looking across to the other side of the garden. Again, Steven tried to see what was there, something that would make her risk falling from the balcony, considering how far she was stretching out over the railings. Again, nothing. A quick glance at Gypsy confirmed that there was nothing. She would have noticed something, if there was something.

That was when the roar came, a faint sound emitting from inside The Chine, growing louder as it echoed out into the grounds. It was violent and threatening, in its entirety. Steven had seen many things and heard just as many in the night. This was a first for him. This was no ordinary ghostly moan; it was a deep, angry explosion —like a final warning. Gypsy sank to the floor, her head resting across her front legs, her big brown eyes looking up at her master.

" OK, we can go back to the house, pitiful thing. I am scared too."

Steven turned and made his way back down the track. Gypsy bounded off in front of him. She stopped every few yards to ensure he was following, barking at him. They reached the Land Rover, and he opened the door for her to jump in. Then he walked around the front, getting in beside her. He stared at his companion as she barked at him. It was as if she was telling him off for making her go to the stupid hotel. Steven reached

109

across to her, only for her to move her head away to the side, her bright, pink tongue flopping out of her mouth as she panted.

"Hey, come on, I said sorry. You do not have to go there again. Friends," he said.

Gypsy turned back to him, lifting her paw and barking at him. She looked happy that they were now sitting in the vehicle. They drove away, heading back to the principal estate. As they made their way, as if human, Gypsy looked in the passenger side mirror, looking at the forest fading away in the distance.

It was just a brief time before Steven was back at The Chine, pulling into the hotel car park. He paused before he turned the engine off. He held the ignition key as he stared ahead, looking across the grounds. It was a strange feeling, being on the grounds. He knew he had to be there for Justyna, even though they were still strangers, yet it was something he knew he had to do. A calling, if you like, a destiny to return to the heart of his roots —amend wrongdoing that had befallen his family.

To say he was not afraid would be a lie. The Chine had scared him for years. Although he was not sure who or what was inside the building, he had seen and heard enough evidence to know it was not friendly. Steven knew that whatever it was, it was watching him as much as he was watching it —almost daring him to come closer — and now he had. It was too late to back out now, so he turned the key, killing the engine, and he stepped out onto the now crispy surface of the snow.

The snow crunched underneath his boots, giving away any surprise he was there, as he walked around the building to the rear gardens.

As he rounded the corner of the west wing, he and Justyna collided into each other. Justyna screamed, jumping back, turning away from him.

"Wow, hey, it's me. It's OK," he said.

Justyna tried to compose herself. "My god. Sorry I screamed — you scared the crap out of me."

"I can tell. I am so sorry," he laughed. "I thought you would have heard me crunching around in the snow."

"What? I heard nothing."

"Well, I parked at the front. I thought you might have heard me pull up."

Justyna looked around, and Steven thought she was not listening to him. He asked her if everything was OK, as she looked worried. It was obvious something was wrong. The Chine. He knew she had seen something, from his earlier observation from the trees. So guessed it was nothing good, judging how Gypsy had reacted.

"Do any families live nearby — with young children maybe?" she asked, still scanning the garden for a sign of something.

"Not around here. Well, not for miles, anyway. Why?"

"I swear I saw a young girl running around the back, running around the gardens."

" OK, when was that? I doubt any local kids would play this far from home, especially here."

"Why not here? That sounded a little forbidden."

"I mean, it is a private hotel. Few kids play in hotels, do they? Plus, like I say, the nearest family home is a long way from here — miles, in fact."

"This sounds crazy, I know, but I saw a child run along that garden hedge, then back along this path to those steps over there."

Justyna pointed to the stairwell leading down to the enormous iron door. Steven looked around, then behind him. He then stepped back, peering around The Chine to where he had parked his vehicle.

"You are aware it has not snowed since about four a.m. this morning, Justyna."

"Yes. What has that got to do with the little girl?"

He looked round them then took her arm, leading her around the side of the building, pointing out his footprints in the snow. Then he led her back to where they bumped into each other, showing her the tracks she had made.

"There are no other tracks, Justyna. If anyone was here, they must have been floating," he laughed.

"Please, I know what I saw," Justyna replied.

She took a smoke from him, as she explained what had happened earlier: the coldness that had swept through her room, the noises, the crying — everything. Steven listened without criticizing or doubting her. They walked around the garden, and she pointed out where she saw the running little girl. Steven pointed out the lack of footprints in the snow, which, in any normal location or situation, would indeed prove an element of doubt.

"Why did you take this job? Did you not ask questions about the property — why it was empty for the winter?" he asked.

Justyna explained her past, and why the job would be a fresh start for her. Her experience in the trade made her the ideal choice for the hotel manager. They continued to talk about her past, her ex being the reason she was here. He explained his history, how he was the heir to the Ballard estate. Steven looked pleased that she was interested in his family background. Not once was money or wealth mentioned. Justyna explained how she would love to go back to the Caribbean and save enough to buy a little café bar. They both seemed relaxed in each other's company. As far as Steven felt, it was an instant attraction from the start. Justyna seemed to feel the same, yet neither would make the first move.

"Hey, come on, let us find this child, then. If you say you saw her, then that is fine by me."

"Great, I thought you may think me crazy or something."

She directed them to the steps leading down to the iron door, saying it was the last place she saw the child go. Steven walked down the steps, suggesting she stay at the top, as the steps were slippery with ice and snow. The door was solid, with two solid bolts, both padlocked. The dirt and rust that caked them showed that they had been locked shut for some time.

"I cannot remember this door, or what they have stored in here. It looks like they have not opened it for some time — it's solid," he said.

"Where did she go, then?" she replied.

She felt cold now, folding her arms and rubbing her shoulders to generate warmth. Steven now stood at the top of the stairwell, looking around, trying to figure out where the door led to. Snow fell, floating down, with no wind to hinder its decent. She had seen something, from his earlier observation from the trees. It was easy to guess it was nothing good, seeing how Gypsy had reacted.

The Chine. "Come on, I have a huge fire in there, calling out my name, and a coffee with yours on it," she said.

This was the dilemma that he had dreaded. If he said no, showing her that he was scared, that would put an end to any chance of getting to know her better. Because he had driven up to the hotel to see her, making an excuse to leave now would be a mistake. If he went into the hotel, the fear would be obvious. Or would it? She had been sleeping there for days now, and no harm had come to her, he thought.

"Well, yes or no? It is getting cold out here. Come on, I promise to behave."

"Well, if that is the promise, I am not coming then," he joked.

His heart ruled his head this time, and he accepted her invitation. As they entered the garden doors to the lounge of the hotel, she asked if he would start the fire. He agreed, and Justyna went off to make the coffee. The fire had just caught as Justyna returned with a tray of coffee and a bottle of brandy.

"We need to talk, Justyna, I need to tell you something."

"Don't tell me you don't drink."

"What, I could drink you under the table; don't worry about that."

"Yeah, I have heard that before. Well, one day we can put that to the test."

"It's this place — it isn't normal. I know you know that, too."

"I suppose it's a bit strange. I mean, on my own I hear things, but they said I would, as its empty. You imagine things, don't you?"

"You really think you're imagining things? When I say I want to tell you something, it is a little bit more than imagination."

"When I arrived, Martin told me the place was haunted."

"He actually said that?"

"Kind of. He hinted that it may be. I think he wanted to say it, but he sort of skirted around it."

The fire was in full flame now, the warmth already heating the lounge. Both sat in front of the fire, leaning forward to each other, there conversation a whisper.

"He did say that if it was not for me, I should leave straight away. Which was odd. And he said something about not looking up at the windows."

Steven stood up, warming his hands in front of the roaring fire. He stooped down, throwing on another log. He looked around the room, knowing somehow that he was not welcome. He was on edge, something that Justyna noted.

"You don't like it here, do you? Is it because of me? Do I make you nervous?" she asked.

"No, not at all. It is not you, believe me. It is this place. It is a bad place, Justyna. Sad things happened here. Old Cupps, the caretaker, was right to warn you off."

"Do not be silly. It is not haunted; it is just a big, empty, old building. Wind, creaks and bangs — they go hand in hand."

"So you have seen nothing, or heard nothing, that seems odd to you? Nothing at all? Come on."

"Haunted by what? Don't be silly."

He knew, as she looked away, her cheeks flushing slightly, that she was lying. Justyna leant forward to pour the coffee, then decided that she wanted a stronger drink. And not Brandy.

"Come on, I want to have a drink. I feel that I may need it, by the sounds of where this conversation is going."

He followed her to the bar, looking around him, his nervousness now on overload. This was as far as he had ever ventured into The Chine. The dark corridors ahead slowed his pace, yet his fondness of his new friend urged him to go with her. As Justyna entered the bar, he stood in the doorway, looking down the corridor to the stairs. He instantly felt the freezing air flowing down the staircase towards him. It was like a slight mist, clouding his view.

As he stepped inside the room, Justyna was standing frozen at the bar, a bottle of Old John in one hand, which she had begun to pour. The dark rum now overflowed from her glass, as it leaked over the bar, dripping to the floor.

"Justyna, the drink! Justyna!" he shouted.

Nothing. She just stared through him, the bottle now empty, yet still in the same position. He took the bottle from her and placed his hand on her shoulders, turning her toward him. He called her name again before she responded.

"Are you OK? You sort of flipped out there, and the rum's all gone."

"What? Did you see him?" she asked. She leant to the side, looking around him as she continued. "The strange man stood next to you."

"Who? It was just me. Look, we have to go — we have to go now, Justyna."

It was too late, as the room became icy cold, their breath clearly visible as they spoke. The bottle at the bar became frosted, as the misty, cold cloud drifted into the room. He took her hand, pulling her from behind the bar, leading her out of the room. It was then that the slight rumble of sound echoed through the hotel — faint at first, before gaining volume and becoming an angry, deep moan. Doors began to open and slam, as the mist became thicker, wisping up into a sinister vapour cone at the front. Justyna stumbled, falling against the wall. She shouted out to Steven, who stopped to help, only to see the reflection of the old lady from the portrait, who had first watched Justyna. She was reaching out, helping Justyna get to her feet. The old lady ushered Justyna along, telling her to run and leave the house. Steven ran back down the corridor, grabbing Justyna's hand, as he stared at the old lady. She smiled at him — a warming, loving smile. He pulled Justyna along the corridor, stopping as he reached the reception. He looked back and saw the cold mist envelope the elderly lady.

His concentration was broken by the booming roar of an angry voice telling him to get out. The thunderous voice filled The Chine. Faintly he could hear crying, screaming children, hiding behind the threatening voice. They both burst out onto the front porch of the hotel, the doors slamming behind them as they stumbled out into the cold.

Beryl Ballard-Young was sat at the window of the library, looking across the estate towards the distant forest, feeling something was not right. No sooner had she felt it than an evil chill surged through her body. The large glass window frosted over before her eyes, as if it was a cold evening's winter's frost. She sipped her tea, turning away from the window to summon Rothman. Beryl knew what was happening. She had expected it — not so soon — but she knew it was coming though, and it was long overdue.

As Rothman entered the room, he felt the chill instantly. "I think the fire needs to be lit, not that it will keep this chill out of the room."

Beryl agreed, watching her butler as he lit the fire. She instructed him to get hold of Father Liam — he was to attend the house as soon as he was able to do so.

Rothman never questioned her. Being in her employ for the past forty years, he knew of the family history. Beryl had entrusted him on various aspects of the family history, letting him read the truth for himself. He had always been loyal to her, not the family. His duty to Beryl was known throughout the family, to the point where she would consult him long before she would her own children. They had faced conflicting times together, and she knew that she could trust him completely, as he did her. He was more than just her butler; he was her confidant.

"Why now? What has caused the unrest?" he asked.

"The girl, perhaps. Steven coming home was always a risk."

"A risk we should have delayed, perhaps."

"No. We both know that I have limited time remaining. I have carried this burden for long enough," she sighed.

"There is always Lady Olivia Jane. Can you not pass this down to her?"

He regretted asking that question as soon as it left his mouth. Lady Olivia Jane, Steven's mother, was only interested in her title and the lifestyle it gave her in the media. As far as the running of the estate was concerned, she was only interested in getting paid her allowance each month. She was happy to let the old lady sort the working side of the estate out.

"Rothman, really. Lady Olivia is the last of our great aristocrats. We both know that she is not the type of person to be confronted with such a task."

"So, it will be down to…"

Beryl finished the sentence for him, knowing perfectly well what name he was about to offer forward. "Steven, yes. Although this girl has a link in this. What that is, I am currently unsure of."

Rothman left to follow out her wishes — contacting the local priest. Father Liam was also known to the family. His involvement with the goings-on at The Chine would prove to be valuable, should things get out of hand.

Justyna climbed into the passenger seat of Steven's vehicle, her hands shaking. She never spoke; she just kept looking across at Steven, hoping he would offer an explanation to what had just happened. Steven just sat looking out of his side window, watching the illuminated windows of The Chine slowly plunge into darkness, as the light from each was diminished.

"We need to get away from here. We're not welcome here," he said softly.

He turned the key, putting life into the engine, pulling slowly away from The Chine. As he began to drive away from the front of the building, Justyna turned to him, screaming at him, demanding to know what had happened. She insisted on knowing who the old lady was, and the man in the mist on the stairs. As tears began to run down her cheek, she suddenly felt scared. She was unsure if she feared the ghosts, or the fact that her disbelief in them had been proved wrong, making her feel stupid.

"Please tell me what the hell is going on. I know what I saw — you saw the same," she said.

"Yes, Justyna, I saw the same as you. An old lady, and the man was Nathaniel Ballard."

"The man from the portrait — he was angry. I could feel it — he wanted to hurt me. I do not know, Steven. I am really confused, and I am scared. Do ghosts hurt people? I mean, in real life. This is real, or is it? It is not like the movies, is it?"

Steven laughed at her innocence — the fact that even though she had seen the same as he had, she was unsure. He told her it was true — all of it. Ghosts were not exclusive to the movies — they did exist.

"Do not laugh at me, please. This is too much to take in. That old woman — was she helping me? Why was she there? Who was she? The shouting — my god. He wanted us to get out, then I heard crying and screaming."

"Hey, come on, calm down; slow down. It will all become clear soon enough."

He drove away from The Chine, all the while watching the hotel in the rearview mirror. Justyna stared at the windows of the hotel as Steven drove away. The light from each window slowly became shrouded in darkness, as did the demons within, who were following them.

"My god, look. Steven, what is going on?" she shouted.

"I know, don't worry, we're safe here. We need to go."

"Go where? What is happening? What did you mean — it will be clear enough? Did you know what was in there?"

Her tone had changed from shock to anger. Steven knew that what he said next would need to be made to sound as if he was as shocked as she had been. He never wanted to lie to her, but if he admitted that he knew the building was haunted, that he had been watching her, she would lose any interest in him —any interest that he hoped she had in him.

"I think I knew something was wrong, but I never imagined it would be like that."

Justyna stared at him, trying to read him. Did he know? She was not so sure. He seemed on edge as soon as he had stepped foot into the lounge. So she asked him again.

" OK, yes, I knew it was haunted. But how do you tell someone new — who you care about — that they are living in a haunted hotel, without them thinking you were mad?"

"You care about me," she said, shocked.

They had reached the estate, so he pulled the vehicle over just inside the gated entrance. As he turned to her, he took her hand, feeling her tremble.

"Yes, I do care about you. Since our first meeting on the beach, I knew you were different. You never asked about my wealth or my title. You just spoke to me like we had been friends for a while."

She sat staring at him, taking in what he had just said. She liked him, yes — he seemed fun. Justyna had hoped he liked her, but considering everything, a romance was not what she had on her mind.

"Isn't this the bit where you say you feel the same way?"

"Oh, I am sorry. Well, yes, of course I like you too. But for now, I just need to know what the fuck is going on. I have been in that hotel for less than a week, and now you tell me you think it may be haunted. I know that, and I hope that wherever you are taking me, they have something to drink."

"Something to drink. Well, as long as you're sure you like me, then... I mean, I don't want you to hold back on how you feel, Justyna."

The silence lasted about ten seconds before they both laughed. Then they sat, looking across at each other. Justyna leant across, cupped his head in her hands and kissed him.

"Of course I feel the same, and I am so glad that you came back to the hotel with me. On my own, I think the outcome would have been far worse."

With that, they drove towards the house. Justyna saw the house appearing in the distance. A large, four-storey, red-roofed Edwardian mansion, square in its design, with a vast driveway. As they drew closer, two large lion statues sat either side of the front steps, proud in their position at the front of the house. The large front windows seemed church-like, high and broken down into smaller-framed glass sections. Steven opened the door, taking her hand and leading her up the concrete steps, up to the large solid oak and metal doors.

"I never normally use this entrance; I just come and go by the rear entrance. Besides, the cook always has something delicious on the go."

"Cook? You have your own cook? Oh, not to lazy, then."

I do not live here; well, not yet, but I will, I guess, eventually."

"Who lives here then? Your parents?" she asked.

"My grandmother lives here. She is the head of the family, then when it is time, she will pass it to me, then I will become Lord Ballard-Young."

"We're meeting your gran? Shouldn't we be speaking to a priest, or some kind of ghost hunter?"

Steven ushered her in the house, shutting the doors behind him. The interior of the house was highly furnished. The floor was decorated with large, black, marbled tiles. That seemed to stretch on forever, as they passed either side of a large, split staircase. Ironically, Justyna's first impression was that it reminded her of an old horror film. As the staircase opened out into a high corridor, she noticed the ornate doors in both directions, spreading out down the upstairs corridors. Huge portraits hung off all the walls, with thick Christmas tinsel draping across the top of them. These were all separated by a range of large, mounted stag heads, again with sparse Christmas decorations hanging from the antlers. An enormous glass chandelier, modern in its design, which illuminated the room perfectly, hung from the high ceiling. Justyna was impressed. It was a beautifully decorated room, which showed a touch of modern and antique tastes.

Suddenly they were interrupted by the barking of Gypsy, as the dog bounded down the staircase, jumping up at Steven. As he struggled to remain upright, he tried to calm her down, only for Gypsy to turn her affections to Justyna. They fussed and petted the loyal dog, who seemed happy they were back safe.

Steven showed Justyna into an adjoining room, the warmth from the room flowing out to meet her. As was Beryl Ballard-Young, leaning forward from her fireside chair, smiling at Justyna. Gypsy, wagging her tail, trotted beside her.

"So, you are the young lady that has managed to catch my grandson's eye. And steal Gypsy from me, I see," she mocked.

Steven took a seat, introducing them to each other casually.

"Really, you want to introduce your friend like that? At least offer Justyna a drink first."

Steven felt his cheeks flush red as he looked at his grandmother, then across to see his guest's reaction.

"Well, I am sure that he has thought about asking me on an official date. Though I feel that he has not quite got his grandmother's bravado," Justyna replied.

"Oh, I like her, Steven. She is very open and direct. She will be perfect for you."

"It is nice to meet you. I am Justyna. I suppose you know what has been happening, regarding The Chine."

"What makes you think I am aware of what has been happening, young lady?"

It was a defensive stance, taken to see what Justyna knew and to try and get her to offer her take on the hauntings. Steven was at the cocktail table making himself a drink, drinking his own in one gulp before offering drinks to the two women. He watched his grandmother, as she watched Justyna, waiting for her to respond to the questioning.

"I guess that, considering what has just happened and that Steven has brought me here, you have more than just an insight to it all. Plus, you have a book with the name Nathanial Ballard written on it, beside your chair."

Justyna nodded towards the book, placed on the table beside the old lady. Beryl smiled once again at her guest, pleased that the girl was at least a little smarter than she expected.

"Are you going to just stand there drinking my whiskey, Steven, or are you going to show some manners and offer the rest of us a drink? Really, my dear, he is quite smitten with you; I have never known him to be so silent."

Gran, please, you are embarrassing her."

"No, Steven, I am embarrassing you," she laughed.

Steven poured them both a drink, not bothering to ask what they preferred, happy to just give them the same as his own. Beryl could see that even though the two were comfortable in their surroundings, there was something that they seemed shaken by. She knew it was The Chine — it was always The Chine. So she pressed for an explanation for them both being at the house without any prior notice.

"Come and sit, my dear girl, Justyna. I like the name — very fresh and modern."

Beryl asked Justyna to sit opposite her, beside the fire. Gypsy had taken up the perfect fireside spot, laid out on the rug in front of the fire. Then Beryl asked her to explain the events that had them so spooked. Between them they explained every detail, from the garden

127

sighting, to the strange old lady stepping out of nowhere to help Justyna to her feet. They left the presence of Nathaniel to the end, where Steven explained the cold that preceded him, along with the demand that they get out.

Beryl sat in silence, letting the two go over the incident, each taking turns to explain what had occurred. They never spoke over each other, both discussing the happenings slowly, with a real fear in their voices. Steven sat on the arm of Justyna's chair, his hand draped across her shoulder.

"The man — the one shouting, angry that we were there — it was him; the man in the portrait. Was it not? Nathaniel," Justyna said.

"Yes, I am afraid so, though he had no qualms with you, Justyna. His anger was vented towards Steven," Beryl replied.

Steven wanted to know why — what had he done to anger some old ghost? But Beryl held her hand up, stopping him from asking more questions.

"Wait, I have asked for Father Liam to come to the house. When he arrives, all will be made clear to you both. Until then, it is pointless me explaining more as I am still unsure of the true facts, other than that we know The Chine is haunted and has been for a long time. A fact that Steven has known as much as I have, Justyna."

Steven jumped up from his chair, shooting his grandmother a look of despair, angry that she should inform his new friend that he had kept the haunting from her. He poured himself another drink, shaking his head in disbelief at his gran's remark. As he looked across at the two women, he caught Justyna staring at him.

"You knew the hotel was really haunted? Proper haunted?" she asked.

"Ever since I was a child, I thought something was wrong, and it was. And now I — we — know it is. But that was why I watched the hotel when you arrived — I wanted you to be safe."

"You watched me? When? Where from?" Justyna asked.

"Oh dear, this is tricky, Steven. Do explain why you watched Justyna."

Beryl was having fun watching her grandson try to wriggle out of his complicated declaration. She rose and went to make fresh drinks for her and Justyna.

"I walked past every night to check on you. After you arrived that wet morning, I just felt drawn to make sure that you were safe."

Beryl took her seat once again, passing a drink to Justyna. She accepted the beverage and winked at the old lady, smiling. Beryl knew that she intended to have fun with her grandson, so she smiled back as she sat back into her fireside seat.

"You mean, you saw me arrive, in that rain, and you were hiding — spying — on me."

"What? No, not spying, I wasn't spying on you. I just wanted to check that you were safe," Steven replied.

"You could have introduced yourself earlier if you were that worried. It sounds like spying to me. What do you think?" she asked Beryl.

"Maybe stalking, at the least."

"Ah, I see. You have known each other, what — twenty minutes — and now you are like best friends, ganging up on me."

"Well, I have to say, at least he was looking out for you. I think the fact that he went into the hotel with you shows how much he likes you, considering how he feels about The Chine and its history," Beryl added.

"Thanks. I think I can big myself up, though. Look, I just know it is an evil place. I have always felt a presence trying to call me, yet warning me to stay away. I have seen things. Nothing like today, but I knew there was something bad in there, waiting."

Beryl stood up and collected the book beside her chair, passing it to Justyna. She suggested that the pair of them get refreshed. She told Steven to take one of the rooms upstairs, suitable for them both. They were to read the book later and get a little background on what The Chine was about. They were to find and understand the reason for Nathaniel Ballard still having not crossed over. Only then would they understand what was in store for them, after they sat and met with Father Liam.

Beryl thought to herself, as she watched the two of them go off to freshen up. The girl, Justyna, seemed very switched on, more than capable of holding her own. She would be good for Steven. It was hard for her to explain to the pair what lay ahead for them, which was why she needed them to meet Father Liam. Together they would explain the history, the truth of The Chine. If the girl was as she expected, then she would not shy away from the role, but would stand alongside Steven as he faced what was about to become the family's dark secret.

CHAPTER 7

Father Liam Parsons was a resolute priest, having followed his religious path since an early age, such was his belief. He had had a desire to go into the church as far back as he could remember. They ordained him into the Order of St Benedict when he reached his late teens. They sent him away to the church of Sant Anselmo all'aventino, in Rome, until his early twenties, instructed by the Vatican to learn a solemn commitment to the church. His Benedictine vow was as a black monk, where he would learn the old 'conversation morum'. This was something rare for the Vatican — an English priest being trained in such a way — as the Benedictine monks were neither clerical nor lay. However, it was possible to be ordained.

For Liam, he was lucky that they agreed to it, and he used his time learning to develop his knowledge and understanding of the deeper, darker side of the church. When he had reached his twenty-third birthday, they positioned him in a role where he had access to the Apostolic Archives. Liam learned all he could, from the trials of the Templar Knights to the marriage requests from Henry Tudor. Liam had an instant attraction to the demonic records, reading from the first church guidelines of exorcism from 1614 to modern-day exorcisms. The records said that over the past ten years, the Vatican had received over 500,000 requests to intervene in demonic possessions. Since 1999, the Vatican had revised its guidelines. They then sent Liam out to shadow a priest, to understand the *De Exorcismis et Supplicationbus Quibusdam*. He was not about to interact or try to involve himself in the exorcisms, only study the cases that were proven to be true demonic possessions and report back to the *Pontifical Athenaeum* on his findings. They had a role for him to fulfil, one they were aware of from an age gone by. Now they had found the perfect person to carry out the church's good work. They would watch and groom him for this role.

Before long, Liam had become a knowledgeable priest, practiced in demonic investigation, rare for such a young priest. With his knowledge of the demonic forces, he was a much-needed priest because of the rise of demonic possessions. As his infamy rose, so did resentment from senior presbyters. After a confrontation with a difficult exorcism, a genuine possession for once, Father Liam had risen to the hype that surrounded him. He had become overconfident, believing his own hype that he was special. After being asked to assist another priest, he lost control of the situation. This time the demon was too strong for such a young inquisitor, and skilled as he was, he had failed to save the girl he was meant to help. The young woman sat up from her bed, bound as she was, her arms stretching tremendously. The voice was so terrible and disturbing that it stopped the priest in his tracks. Then, without questioning, the demon revealed its name openly. This revelation stopped Father Liam in his tracks, confused as to why the demon gave his name freely. His fellow priest begged Father Liam to continue, but the demon sent the assistant sprawling into the wall, knocking him unconscious. Father Liam watched as the demon raised the woman's head, turning to look at him. Then the woman's black lips parted as she whispered to him, green bile pouring from her mouth.

"Abaddon, Father, I am one of many. Your God has used you, played you to do his bidding like a slave, as he left Nathaniel."

Father Liam stepped back, confused, as the demon, Abaddon, laughed through her. The restrains broke, snapping her free, as the trembling priest tried to gather his thinking. How did this woman — this demon — know of Nathaniel? His thoughts were broken again, by the voice of his oldest friend, Beryl.

"Liam, why did you leave? We were friends. Help me — help us."

"You are not her, you are not her. Be gone, evil creature."

"You are no priest. You want to fuck her — your old friend. God knows, and he despises you. You are a worthless, faithless fraud."

He held his bible up towards the woman, hoping to find his place. Before he could regain his position, the demon began laughing once more.

"Fool, we do not need this worthless body; her soul is nothing to us. We will meet again soon enough, priest. We are waiting and watching."

Then the woman held her free arms up to her head, and with a sudden twist, snapped her own neck, leaving the body crumpled forwards on the bed.

They sent him back to England as soon as he had rested, where he would serve his old diocese. He would be answerable only to the Cardinal, head of the church in London, where he would be the overseer in any such investigations into possessions across the British Isles, sparse as they were. Even then, Liam had worries of the past, and he was aware that the Vatican would not leave the issue closed. The conclave were optimistic for Father Liam Parsons. They were sure that when he was ready, he would face his demon, and only then would he return home to the Vatican. What state of mind he was in, remained to be seen.

They quizzed him on his knowledge of his home parish. They asked him what he knew of the history of the area and if he had met any of the earlier priests. They wanted to know how close he was to Beryl and her family. Then, when they were sure he was ready, they began telling him the true story of The Chine: why they needed him to return, and to wait and watch over The Chine. He began to understand why this demon had attached itself to him, as if it were aware of his connection to the Ballard family. So they sent him to succeed a line of earlier priests who were sworn to keep the secret hidden and protect the Ballard's. Of course, he would accept, his old friend now being the head of the family. Deep down, he was more concerned that the demon knew of her.

He had been in the Dorset region now for twenty years. The Vatican claimed that as this was his own region, he would, in time, be invaluable to the secret the church held over the region. As he declared he knew the Ballard family so well, it would be good to have a priest who had the respect of the family, along with the friendship of the head of the family. Father Liam already knew of the ghostly rumours at The Chine, plus the sightings were getting more frequent. He never understood why they never just closed it down and built some farm building over the site. No questions would be asked, and no land would be disturbed. However, this was not his concern — he had no say in such matters. His opinion was just that.

It was well documented. He had been informed to report any news to his superiors. And plus, as a boy, he had seen things too. This was a long time ago though; it was obvious now why they were sending him home. They often asked him to investigate the mental state of various people; Latin families, who were convinced that demons owned a member of the family. But Father Liam would find out that the families were often migrants whose children had found a new way of life — a life involving drugs and drinks, and nothing to do with demonic forces. It was rare that he had any cause for concern about such dark forces. In fact, he had none. Hauntings may have been true for a few select locations, where he would bless the house, cleansing it. They did this more for the peace of mind of the owners, not to challenge any ghosts.

Father Liam read constantly, searching for any information on his own demon, researching items passed across to him from the Vatican. The Chine was not a normal haunting, though, and he was no fool. He knew that the Vatican were slowly building him back up, getting him back in the game, ready for the demon he was sworn to face.

The call from Rothman was not a surprise. Father Liam knew The Chine would reveal its secrets soon. He had hoped that it would not be in his time, though, skilled as much as he was. Father Liam knew that this demon was waiting for him or seemed to be waiting for something. Beryl had mentioned the history often to him. He knew she had been passed on the knowledge from her family, as they all had done throughout the years. The parish diaries had further information, yet there was still a deeper element that only he was aware of.

Father Liam looked up from his books as he sat alone in his study. An icy chill gripped him like a vice. He drew a deep breath, crossing himself, as he looked at the cross above his desk. It was a long time coming, and he knew that the voices he heard in his head were beckoning him to enter The Chine. Often, when he slept, visions would haunt his dreams. Even when he was walking along the quiet country roads, visiting his parishioners, the voices would whisper to him. Now he knew he had to face it — he had to confront the demon, Abaddon. There was no other way. The sudden appearance of Steven and this girl had brought things to a head.

He packed the parish diaries into his satchel and readied himself to see his dear friend, Beryl.

As he reached the end of the garden at the front of his cottage, Father Liam looked back up the path. Perfect whitewashed walls covered the cottage, surrounded by a variety of climbing plants that reached the upper windows. They twisted and wrapped around the window trellises, the bright red and yellows highlighted against their white background. Mixed with the purple and blue of the climbing clematis, the cottage could be a blueprint for any biscuit or toffee tin, a perfect picture for a postcard. The path he had laid all those years ago, edged with white stone from the Portland quarry, stretched away to the large oak door ahead of him. It was his hidden retreat, a place to relax and read, away from the torment that his role had created for him: the nights of constant whispering, echoing throughout the cottage; demonic voices — abusing him, challenging his beliefs, pushing him to the edge of reason. It was his choice, though; Father Liam had been aware of the cost, should he follow his path to demonic pursuance. The priests may cast demons out of a body. This does not mean they disappear. They want their revenge. Their voices were clear to the priests once they stepped into their darkness. Their voice haunted the priests for years to come. Only the sanctuary of the church would protect them. So they often remained in the church's safety for the rest of their lives.

It bothered him not that he was leaving. Father Liam knew how to deal with the whispering insults — the threats that awaited him were different. God would protect him — this he was sure about. His faith never waned. It was his strength to go head-to-head, which may drain him. That was his only concern. Only the promise of returning to the sanctuary of the Vatican gave him hope. One last challenge, and then he could rest. With that thought, Liam smiled, a big smile of content. The priest knew that this was the last time he would set foot in the garden. Never would he be returning to his quaint cottage. After this, he was going home to Rome, to the Vatican, where he would spend the rest of his days. Stepping foot into The Chine was always going to be the end for him. His exorcisms never worried him, as he knew God would protect those who had faith. Demons would be cast out. The ghosts of The Chine would be put to rest. The demons in The Chine were a mixture of demonic force, black magic and pure hatred. Unlike an exorcism, where the demon is using a host for its own purpose, The Chine harboured a range of ghostly apparitions, trapped and tortured by their host —all angry and searching for an out. Over time, the demon had taken them, forcing them to reach out and attach themselves to anyone who dared to come across them. Now it was time to use every ounce of his energy and skills to free them, a task that would normally exhaust and drain any priest. This time, he was not going alone.

Father Liam closed the garden gate, taking one last look at his cottage. He had sent word back to the Vatican, detailing what he was preparing to do. He then lifted his bicycle from the garden wall, installing his books into the wicker basket, and made his way along the track heading towards the manor.

Steven and Justyna were sitting on the large double bed in one of the master bedrooms. Steven was just out of the shower. A large bath towel was draped around his waist; he dried his hair with a smaller towel. He was walking around the room, chatting to Justyna about the events from earlier.

Justyna had other thoughts running through her head. "Sorry to interrupt you, Steven, but do you think your grandmother, Beryl, thinks we are a proper couple? You know, dating and all that."

"I do not know — why?"

"Duh, the double room. She considers we are, shall we say, sleeping together, it seems."

"Well, I suppose so, yes. I can grab another room — it's fine. I never thought about it, to be honest. With what has happened, I just never thought about the sleeping arrangements."

"So we're sleeping together now, are we?"

"What? No, I just meant…"

Justyna started laughing, cutting his conversation dead. Steven realized she was winding him up again. Justyna explained she had no qualms about sharing a room. She looked happy that she would not be alone. He rubbed his damp hair as he sat on the bed beside her, resting his hand on her knee.

"Well, I wanted to ask you out — for dinner or something. We have jumped well ahead of that conversation, don't you think?" he said.

"So it seems. Besides, it cuts out all the awkward flirting or any silly conversations."

"Silly? Why would we have any silly conversations, Justyna?"

"You know — what is your favourite band, colour. Do you like Chinese food —that silly stuff."

He laughed at her directness, the way she just cut through the chase —direct to the point. Steven liked that about her. He stood looking at her, as she changed into the warm clothes she had found in the wardrobe. Justyna then stood admiring herself in the wardrobe mirror, impressed that the clothes were a good fit. As she smiled at her reflection, she noticed Steven staring, transfixed on her. She walked over to him, watching his cheeks flush, as he realized what he had been doing. Justyna placed her arms around him as she kissed him on the lips. After a short while, they pulled apart, smiling at each other, their arms dropping to their sides. They held hands as they looked at each other.

"I am so glad you 're safe. Also, I am glad that you are here. Here with me. I hope that after all this mess, you will stay, Justyna."

"I think I would like that; though, let's get this nightmare sorted first, shall we? Then you can ask me."

This was how they left the conversation as, arm in arm, they left the room to see what Beryl and her clergy friend had to say. They made their way downstairs to meet the waiting pair. A hundred or more questions were flashing through Justyna's head. There were so many things that needed explaining, yet she was unsure that she was ready for the explanations that were waiting.

The house seemed eerie now. As they descended the stairs, every portrait had an ancestor who glared out at her, watching her as she passed. Justyna gripped Steve's arm tight, pulling him to her. They reached the study room, and Steve reached out to open the door.

"Are you ready for this? I do not know what they want to say to you, or us, but I feel it will be to do with that shithole hotel."

"Steve, I think we both know what to expect after what we saw in The Chine. Whatever they say it was, it will not be great, will it? Plus, this is just the beginning, for both of us."

"You think we are going back to the hotel?" he asked her.

"You know we are."

He did know, however it was something he felt had to be asked to make sure they were both in harmony . The thought had crossed her mind that she should just leave to go back to London. It was a brief thought, as she knew her future lay here now. For some strange reason, she knew she had to see this through to the end. A calling, if you like.

CHAPTER 8

Every corner of the snow-covered road seemed worse than the last, as the compact car struggled to keep its traction at each turn. For the driver, Edyta, feeling tired from the long drive, this was an added struggle.

Edyta was Justyna's oldest friend, having left Poland to look for work in the UK over twelve years ago. They had both been through rough times along the way. However, they had come through it all now. They each had good jobs, even suitable careers. Edyta had gone into teaching, where her friend had chased her dream to work around the world, even managing the best hotels in the most luxurious locations. Yet, they always stayed in touch. Not daily, though more than enough to remain the best of friends.

Edyta had an Eastern Bloc beauty: high cheekbones, tall, and long hair, always bunched up and pulled back. She had eyes that saw through any chancer. She had brains and beauty and was sporty-looking, even though she would rather sit in her kitchen with a bottle of wine than do any sport. Yet, like her friends, she looked fit and healthy.

As she had not heard from her friend, knowing that Justyna expected her to come down and see her, the chance to just turn up and surprise her was a great idea. Besides, she wanted to see that she was coping after the split from her ass of an ex.

Soon they sat nav had dropped, the connection gone. Snow was again falling, thicker now. She had to be close. For Christ's sake, she had been driving forever, it seemed. The decision to stop and walk was a brave one. It seemed better to walk the rest of the way than the need to get the car recovered from a roadside ditch hidden by the snowdrifts. Although she had not dressed for the harsh weather, she braved the elements, as she was sure the hotel was not far away.

It was not long before The Chine came into view. The enormous towers of the hotel were just visible through the falling snow, away in the distance. After a few slips and falls — nothing too tragic — Edyta reached the hotel rear gate. The gate had a large padlock, securing it for the winter, so she threw her small suitcase over then clambered after it. After a short walk, she arrived at the front of the hotel. It was dark — not a single light was on. She remembered Justyna said she had a room in one of the tower rooms overlooking the rear garden. Edyta stepped back into the snow, looking up at the corner tower after working out which room it was. Then the lights in the room came on, and a shadow crossed behind the window.

"That must be her — nice and warm while I am out here freezing my tits off."

She shouted up at her, sure that she would hear her in the silent evening. The wind carried her voice away, as she continued to shout out. Shouting turned to cursing, as one light went out and was replaced by another.

"Drunk, I expect. I knew I should have called her first," Edyta muttered to herself.

As she walked back under the cover of the hotel canopy, she noticed the door was ajar. With her case in her hand, she nudged the door further open and peered inside. It took a while for her eyes to adjust to the darkness inside, but as they did, she ventured further in. She stamped her feet on the coconut welcome mat and shouted out.

"Hello! Justyna! Hey, it is me, and I am freezing cold. Hello. Where are the bloody lights in this place?"

As she felt along the wall, searching for a switch, she heard the laughing drifting down the dark hallway to her left. Her hand felt the switches on the wall. She flicked them all on. The hotel remained in darkness, much to her dismay. Again, laughter echoed through the darkness. She turned back to leave the lobby, only for the door to slam shut before her.

"Hey, hello, I am a friend of Justyna. Is she here? The lights are not working. Hello, is someone there?" she asked.

The door would not open, no matter how hard she tried to pull at the handle. Her back now against the door, she stood looking around the room, trying to see into the dark.

"If that is you playing games, I will bloody kill you, Justyna. Stop messing about. Where are you?"

She could hear whispering from along the hall, so now feeling angry, she walked down the hall towards the hotel bar. Halfway along the hallway, the light from behind the bar came on, giving the bar entrance a slight glow. Convinced her friend was in the bar playing games, she continued along the hallway.

"Well, I hope you have a drink waiting for me. It is bloody winter outside. No wonder you 're staying in the bar."

As she turned into the bar, expecting to find her friend, it confused her to find it empty. She walked up to the bar, peering over the counter, finding nothing and nobody. The room went cold, her breath visible as she exhaled. Edyta knew she had to leave. She had seen enough horror films to know when it was time to leave. She turned around, only to see the old lady in front of her. Her hand pointed towards the door, her face, even in its ghostly state, saddened.

"Run, child, get away! He is coming for you. Run while you still can."

Edyta fell sideways, terrified. Her hand reached up to the bar, and she pulled herself back up. The old lady again warned her to go, but Edyta's legs were shaking. It was impossible for her to run. As she stumbled away to the door of the bar, she crashed against the chairs and

147

tables, trying to keep her balance. The ghostly figure of the old woman tracked beside her, still urging her to flee.

Edyta wanted to know who was coming, yet she could not get the words out. So she tried to compose herself, regain her balance and leave the bar. She made it to the hallway, looking over her shoulder. She could still see the ghostly apparition of the old lady in the bar doorway, pointing towards the lobby as it looked back down the corridor towards the staircase.

As she felt along the panelled walls, Edyta tried to make her way along, only to be stopped in her tracks by a booming roar. Fear forced her to look back towards the bar, where she saw a thick, black haze flowing toward her, the coldness ripping into her as it slammed against her. She stood with her eyes closed, hoping it was all a dream. After a few seconds, she opened her eyes, looking down the hall to the bar and stairs. Whatever it was, it had gone, and so had the old woman. For a short few seconds, she thought it was all tiredness, lack of sleep and her imagination.

As she squinted into the blackness, the apparition of Nathaniel Ballard merged from the darkness behind her, drifting from one side of her shoulder to the other, studying her menacingly. His dark, hollow eyes were pure evil in the surrounds of his pale skin. From behind her, away in the distance, the lounge piano played. Edyta turned her head to look toward the sound of music, only to be met by the haunting image of

Nathanial. Then the hotel plunged into darkness once more, as the terrifying screams of Justyna's best friend filled the air. She was carried away, levitating through the darkness, as if she was dangling on a string like a puppet. Her body began slamming into the walls, her limp limbs smashing against the furniture, as if a puppet master had lost control of the strings to one of his toys. Blood was splattering everywhere, across the floor, running down the walls, her bones breaking as her body was battered and hurled from side to side along the black hallway. The sound of sickening thuds was dominated by deranged laughter.

As Edyta's body disappeared into the dark fog, battered from what seemed like a mixture of assailants, The Chine was silent once more as the pandemonium began fading away. As soon the dark, black fog dispersed, the sound of children drifted through the lower floors of The Chine. This time, the laughter was replaced by crying. The sound was flowing along in the dark, as if the children were running down the staircase. Each sprinting step was heard, as the sound carried down the stair carpet, heading towards the reception. Then, as soon as it began, it faded away, and once more The Chine fell silent and darkness took over.

Outside, the snow was falling thicker and faster now. Shrieking winds flowed around the building, gusting around the walkways. The bright, full moon began to cast wavering shadows from the giant pines, across the white, carpeted floor, as their canopies rocked in the breeze. Drifts began to steep at the side of the building, reaching up to the windowsills, as the glass began to frost. The chilly air was nothing compared to the coldness that was building inside The Chine. The demon that controlled the lost soul of Nathaniel Ballard, waited, knowing what was coming.

CHAPTER 9

It was early evening. Father Liam had arrived and took his seat beside the fireside, next to Beryl. Steven and Justyna, having been introduced to the priest, were now sat at the desk at the far end of the room. They were reading the book as instructed by the priest, as Beryl had mentioned earlier. It was the true facts about the horrific past of Steven's family history. They read in silence, as they both began to understand what had happened all those years ago.

Father Liam smiled. He knew the girl was no dummy. He studied her from his chair. she was not just reading the history; she was learning it, storing as much knowledge as she could. He rose from his chair, walked up to Justyna and placed his hand on her shoulder. Justyna looked up at him, a question already forming on her lips

"Finish what you are reading, my child. We can sit together and discuss what we all know. Only then will I be able to answer you. So I can plan what needs to be done."

Once more, his tone was soothing. He returned to his seat and continued his hushed conversation. It was clear, no matter what was to be decided. As he had said to Justyna, it was down to him to decide. No one else noticed the comment. They were oblivious to his reckoning. Father Lian, Beryl and Rothman sat by the fire, discussing matters relating to The Chine. Demolish the hotel or lease it out again? They all agreed that, as it stood, it could no longer function as a hotel.

The book was more of a diary; it explained a lot of detail about the family. They added new entries as time went by, from various heads of the family. Steven felt they seemed to act like a secret sect —a hidden family within a family. Only the heads of the family knew the history —information passed down the family tree —all hiding secrets from the rest.

As they read on together, keeping pace with each other, the dark side of Nathaniel formed. The logbook explained how the slaves never adapted to life on the estate. Cold winters were not for them. Snow was something that they never had to deal with. All the estate slaves, Petersen, Ricard and Evens, looked content, as they were free to roam the grounds. Not happy, just content. Rosaline and Jaddine were not used to the kitchen facilities and were often being scolded by the cook. As for Lovelie, she tried to fit in as a house servant much to the anger of her mistress. It was a hard struggle to get things correct or in order. They scolded Emanuel and Junior. They were always in the way, making the day-to-day chores chaos. The estate staff found the slaves entertaining and bonded a little. They would joke with the older men and ask them question after question, just to hear them talk, finding even that funny. They all noticed that when the young Emanuel was nearby, they fell silent, looking away. The book said that when anyone made conversation with the young child, he never tried to further the conversation, he just nodded in agreement. Yet he watched them, from a window or from the corner of the building. Watching and listening, making the other slaves nervous and on edge.

It seemed a short while after returning that Anabelle became ill. She escaped to the estate, from London, as the bad air theory was rife. She had consumption, so they deemed a time spent at the estate ideal for her health. They often sent Emanuel to her room with a glass of port and jelly. So as her health worsened, he was Nathaniel's' scapegoat, beaten more often, as Nathaniel's love became frail. Workers complained the boy was being mistreated, only to be told that if they disliked the way they ran the estate, they were welcome to leave their cottages and find work elsewhere.

Leandro was soon back on the estate to comfort his friend. He heard from the staff that they often saw the slaves rallying around the young boy. After this news reached Nathaniel, he chastised all the slaves. Only the cook, Ms Wynn, stood up to the master. She, herself, had once complained to Nathaniel that the slaves were, in fact, useless, and that they caused more work, often ruining the cooking by burning or dropping the food.

153

She said that consumption was common amongst the women of London, and that Anabelle needed rest and fresh air, not to be shut away in her room like a leper.

The two read on further, and it was later revealed that poor Anabelle had died, weak and pale. When she tried to converse, she coughed, spitting blood and phlegm. Her thin, weak body was nothing like Nathaniel remembered of her. He at first blamed his friend, Leandro, for bringing the disease back from the trade routes. He then changed his opinion and blamed the slaves for being carriers.

His mood changed. He became drunk daily and abusive to all. Leandro told the estate ground workers to go home, stay at home with their families and to stay safe, because of the disease. Reading between the lines, though, it was plain to see that they said this to keep prying eyes away from the mistreatment of the slaves. Only Ms Wynn remained working at the estate.

The next entry in the book was some two weeks later. By now, Nathaniel was drunk daily. His fighting with Leandro was a common event. He kept the slaves in an underground garden storage bunker. Ms Wynn would take food to them without his knowledge.

Anabelle's parents took her body to be buried at home, much to the anger of Nathaniel. He refused to speak to them. He was adamant that a curse was upon her, either by the slaves or by a jealous friend. It was then that, as he paced up and down Anabelle's room, he saw Ms Wynn taking food to the gardens. In a rage, he flew down to meet her on her return, followed by Leandro. In the kitchen, he roared at her for betraying his trust and accused her of having something to do with Anabelle's demise. She called him cruel and stupid. As she turned her back on him, he grabbed a large, cast-iron pan and smashed it across the back of her head. She was dead before she hit the floor. Laughing at the dead woman, he smashed the pan into her head, over and over. Nathaniel kicked at her lifeless body, pointing at her, telling Leandro that she did it — her and the slaves. It was then that Nathanial said that the slaves needed to go. Nathaniel's plan to dispose of the slaves and the cook were different from Leandro's. His idea was to take them to London by boat and sell them on as crew to another seafarer. They could dump the cook's body at sea on the way, saying she fell overboard for some reason. Nathanial wanted to dump the dead cook's body in the bunker along with the slaves, then wall them all in. This plan was one that Leandro was not comfortable with, yet he went along with his friend's plan about the slaves but managing to change Nathaniel's mind about the cook.

Then one dark, Autumn night, the deed took place. The two men had returned to the house, and Nathaniel opened a bottle to celebrate the demise of his love's killers. Soon the estate workers began asking where the slaves had gone. They could not have been moved off the estate with no one knowing. In a close community, the local workers and the wives missed nothing. People

155

talked of murder and sad things happening at The Chine. Influential people were asking questions, to which a drunk Nathaniel and his secretive friend, Leandro, rebuked.

Soon after a trip to London, Nathaniel found he was no longer welcomed in his circle of associates. They warned him that things were being spoken about him. Not good things, so once more, in a rage, he returned home to The Chine, Leandro in tow trying to console him. Before long, Nathaniel began once again to blame Leandro for bringing the slave's home. Leandro, now despising his friend, informed Nathaniel that Anabelle and Ms Wynn's death were down to him. Raged at the gall of such a claim, Nathanial took a knife from his table and plunged it into the back of his once friend, stabbing him over and over. The following day, as he stumbled around the house, he found his friend's body heaped on the floor at the dining table. It hit him that he had gone too far and that he could not dismiss the body — another body. People were already talking about the mystery of the cook and the slaves. His own family had warned him he needed help. What use would they be to him now? They would not help him.

It was weeks before his family came to check on Nathanial, having not heard from him. They found him hanging in Anabelle's bedroom. The body of his friend lay at the foot of the stairs. A search of the grounds revealed the underground storage room, but no slaves, nor the cook. One of the gardeners revealed that the room seemed smaller. It was not hard to figure out what had happened.

Shocked and dismayed at the thought of what lay behind the newly built wall, the family decided that the family name needed to be protected from what had Nathanial had done. So they took The Chine, and they put the estate back to work. Any embarrassment that had occurred was hushed up to save a scandal. As the estate was a gift from the crown, they saw any connection with the antics of a deranged madman to be unacceptable. So the Victorian powers that be had the whole affair covered up. Nathaniel Ballard had died at sea, along with his trusted captain. They would hang portraits of the man in The Chine's hall, showing the man at his best. The grounds would remain in the family name, and the farms would be extended, creating more jobs in the area. And the heath and coastal areas would become a place for all to visit, not just for health reasons.

Senior members of the Ballard family agreed never to develop The Chine or its grounds. The past would remain that. They drew plans up for a new manor house. The farm and worker cottages would move to the far end of the estate. The Chine was now a listed building, and the lease would run for as long as there was a Ballard alive to support the secrecy.

After they finished reading, they looked at each other, Steven shaking his head in disbelief. Justyna asked him how this stayed a secret. Over time, it had to come to the surface.

"The Chine was empty for so long, according to my grandmother," Steven whispered.

"But it is horrendous. How can a family keep such a secret, even passing this on? I know families have ties and history. Yet, this is just taking things too extreme," she replied.

"I knew we were slavers back in the day. I swear, this is all news to me."

"Of course it is. They passed it down from family elder to the next in line. Was she going to tell you about this, even if the hotel was not such a creepy, haunted place?" she asked.

"She knew I was against the family's history regarding our slave trade, even if it was generations ago. I always said we should come clean. I mean, not that we are the only wealthy family who made money back in those days. Half of England's wealth in those dark days was born out of the slave trade."

They looked across at the others, who were now all staring at them. His grandmother was first to speak, as Father Liam once again filled his glass, pouring refills for the two younger members of the room.

"I understand your, shall I say, unpleasantness, at what happened all those years ago. And yes, the house remained empty for many a year. Untouched. The bodies remain where he disposed of them."

"How? The staff, or the farm workers, they knew. The book says they asked and doubted his story."

"My son, back in the day, the lord of the manor was just that. You worked for the family; they did not expect you to question or disagree. The proprietors of the day had substantial power and respect. Those people bowed their head and tugged their forelocks. Rumours were abound yet never followed up on," Father Liam replied. He passed the two their drinks and invited them to join them, pulling extra chairs up to the fireside.

"So the church has known about this and not intervened?" Justyna asked.

"We know many things, not all good. Yes, we helped the family in its time of need. We also were part of the coverup. You must understand, history changes rapidly. The church understood the need to step in and take sides, for reasons only known to the church conclave."

"You mean, for its greater good; like land, and power over influential people. Favours in return," Justyna replied.

"Ah, yes. I remember you have been here, talking with my grandmother. The family donations, large donations to the church —all this is a payoff for your silence," Steven said to Father Liam.

"I cannot say the church has been honest in all their beliefs, nor can I say they are wrong. Whatever helps God's work — no matter how devious we carry it out

— it is what it is. Sometimes dark work needs to be done to make the world safe from evil."

Father Liam told them how the Catholic church had appointed a black priest in America in the mid 1800's. A former slave himself. They even took him to Rome to study. Even though many Catholic regions condemned such a bold move, the Vatican remained strong in their appointment. As ever, nobody dared challenge the decision. Imagine the backlash should the news of the dead slaves escape out into the world. So it was agreed that they keep this under their own protection for a while, until it was considered safe to correct."

"Perhaps, but it had been a secret for longer than was needed, I think," Steven added.

The priest smiled at the boy, nodding in agreement. It was true. He could not deny it had been covered up for too long.

"So much happened soon after — much more — faster than was expected. With the slaver abolished, black communities were cropping up everywhere. Great migrations were occurring across the globe. The Vatican saw slight difference in the liturgy of spiritual patrimony."

"So you're saying, to keep the black communities on the Vatican's side, it was brushed aside for longer. That is absurd," Justyna replied.

"Well, before long, innovators like Father Clarence Rivers, began integrating Negro spirituals into his mass, and the whole thing blossomed into the black Catholic movement. Then, in the '60s and '70s, with black power, it was not the time to question what Nathaniel Ballard had done. It was better to keep it in your family and keep the land as it is today."

"And keep the Vatican safe from any fallout from the now growing black community," Justyna sighed.

"But you knew this day was coming, didn't you?" Steven asked.

"Perhaps, perhaps not," Father Liam replied.

"Then how come an inquisitor has remained here in lowly Dorset, when your work across Europe is more important? I read that, in Italy, there had been over four hundred requests for exorcisms," Justyna asked.

"Why would a young girl from your background know of such things? What knowledge do you have of the sacraments of the church?" the priest asked.

"I read an article once, at an airport, that the Pontifical Apostolorum, or something, were training priests in demonology."

Steven looked shocked that she knew about such things. She caught him staring at her.

"I missed a flight once, in Rome, on a connecting flight. I found a magazine. I was bored, so I read it."

"Interesting that you should recall it," Father Liam said. Father Liam knew the girl was not stupid, but he was shocked that she had knowledge of such things. She had a deeper connection to the events surrounding The Chine.

As she continued, he listened to her explain what she understood about demonic possessions; how she thought that the church had stepped up its belief in true demon possession. Justyna told them she found it odd, as the current Pope appeared more modern in his beliefs, declaring the devil was an actual person, armed with dark powers.

Laughing, Father Liam congratulated her on what she knew. He also informed her she should not believe all she read.

"The devil is ecumenical. All churches have seen the need for deliverance from such dark infestations."

"Good grief, so you are saying that demons are everywhere? It is not just a catholic thing?" Steven asked.

"Of course not. Look, Satan is real, and not only that, but he is also more powerful now than ever before. TV and films have promoted his power tenfold."

Father Liam sat relaxed in his fireside chair. He had discussed these questions a thousand times before this night. People always seemed interested in the dark side of religion. If only the same was for God, then the churches would be full.

"Films like 'The Exorcist' and all those devil films, help to increase people's interests in the occult. I hope you believe us when we say that the dark side is just that. It has always been here," Beryl added.

Father Liam stood and walked over to Steven and Justyna. He knelt before them, his hand resting on the arm of Stevens' chair, helping to steady himself.

"The new world has rediscovered a whole new realm of the supernatural. The church, mine and others. No matter how conservative we coat it, it has enabled the devil, as the New Testament puts it, to prowl around the darkness like a lion, looking to devour whoever he wants."

"Brilliant, and you want us to go back into the hotel to face him. Sorry, excuse my French, but you can fuck off," Steven shouted.

"I doubt that the devil himself will be there, babe," Justyna told him

"No, well, his minions will be, as we already know. We met them earlier."

Steven downed his drink in one gulp and paced around the room. He informed the room that the book was a court case waiting to explode. It would drag the family name through the mud —much as they deserved it, too.

"The book said that Nathanial bricked the slaves in. So the little child I saw and heard — I take it that was one of them?" Justyna asked.

"Oh, without doubt. Plus, the laughter you heard — that would be them also," Rothman answered.

"Then why do they sound so happy? I would have thought they were the angriest out of all the ghosts," Justyna said.

"I cannot say why they are happy, or if they are. Though in past multiple possessions I have dealt with, these secondary sightings often antagonize the demonic beings, knowing that their time is limited."

"Now you're telling us that ghosts dislike each other and have a pecking order," Steven complained

"Steven. Stop being so silly. We need to sort this out and end it. Now, tomorrow, or whenever. You need to set this right. I am as scared as you, and I do not believe in ghosts," Justyna said.

"Oh, I do like her," Beryl whispered.

"Yes, I know. I am furious, Gran, that you knew all this. The entire history. I knew The Chine was an evil place. I saw things as we all did, as everyone did. But why now? What has called this mad, old, pirate slaver to get angrier?"

"Because you're back — the new heir to what was his estate," Justyna replied.

"She is right. In a way. They cut Nathaniel off from his family — our family. They stripped everything he created for his future, from him. His love taken from him. Whatever sanity he had left died when he turned on his staff and his friend. Suicide was a sin, and he saw that as his only release," Rothman said.

Rothman rose and took the logbook from the table, putting it back on the bookshelf. He explained the family informed the church long ago of what had happened. Even back then, the belief in demons was strong, more so than today, as people were a God-

164

fearing group. More people attended church than modern day times. So the church had great concern that a waiting evil had already marked his soul.

He took his seat once more, and Father Liam continued his warning for him.

"Even though we knew, or someone in the diocese knew, to conduct such an evil doing, you had to be pure evil. Which Nathaniel Ballard was not; well, before the loss of Anabelle, he was not. Somewhere along the way, he was getting depressed — angry — over the slave's actions. He forgot why they were there."

"I know you think it wrong that we hid the genuine history of the family from you, Steven. This was a dark family secret. One that could disgrace us all, even now."

"So you decided long ago to do nothing, Gran. Those slaves, their bones left to rot in that bunker. They should have cleared them away long ago," Steven informed her.

"I agree, of course I do. However, nobody has the keys to that bunker, nor does the hotel have the right to any access to it. Soon it was too late to just walk in there and claim it back," Beryl answered.

"We decided they were best left untouched, until a time came to lay them to rest — like now," Father Liam replied.

He reached across to Beryl, taking her hand, assuring her she had done no wrong

"No matter what the reasons were, the past is just that. We must deal with what is now. You can decide who is to blame after we face this demon," he told them.

"Amazed as I am, and as great as that sounds, Father, I am not too happy at facing anything in that place, after what we saw on the last trip."

"Steven, this has been brewing for some time. He knew you were here, and he wanted you to enter his domain. Not Nathaniel. He is just an empty vessel, used by this evil. The second you crossed the threshold of The Chine, you gave his demon more power. Nathaniel's hatred of his kin, for the way they cast him aside, has fuelled the darkness to flow from him, spreading further afield. You have seen nothing yet," the priest said.

After he lost Anabelle, his life spiralled out of control. He only saw the negative impact. Prior to this, as a mariner, he was a God-fearing man. In the end, he was a muttering alcoholic mess. Murder and self-loathing was his only companion," Beryl added.

"So his misery was a gift to the dark forces then," Justyna replied.

"Sadly, yes. Now I need to face it, and I need your help — both of you."

"Should we set the slaves free first, or whatever it is you are meant to do?" she asked.

"Of course, they have a part to play in this too. The fact that they roam the grounds and the hotel, proves they can somehow torment this entity."

"Wait, Justyna, are you sure you want to return to The Chine? This is not really your issue; you can wait here. In all honesty, I do not want to go, either."

She laughed at him in a slight manner. She looked around the darkened room, as they all sat illuminated from the fire glow. They all held her gaze, smiling at her. For once she felt she belonged somewhere. Steven's grandmother liked her; she knew this from the start. The priest seemed sincere, as if he would protect them no matter what happened. Plus, she felt the children — the slaves at The Chine — wanted her to help. Even the old lady — the ghost of the cook. It dawned on her that it was her in the restaurant that morning, watching over her.

"What do you suggest we do, Father? Of course we will come with you."

"We will?" Steven asked her.

Her look was all he needed to agree, although he still felt angry that his grandmother had brough him home purely for this reason. He sat, shaking his head at the old lady.

"Gran, you really are devious. I will be surprised if a demon isn't waiting for you."

The rest of the evening was spent discussing how they would approach The Chine. There was no point in creeping around the back of the building; the element of surprise was not needed. So they agreed, Steven reluctantly, to just walk in the front door. Father Liam had all he needed with him.

He later confided to Beryl that he would be going back to Rome; the Vatican would be expecting him. Beryl knew that this would be the last time he faced up to any dark forces. For him, his duties would be over. She would never see her friend again.

Rothman showed the father to his room for the night, before making sure his mistress and her guests had all they needed for the rest of the night. Then he dismissed himself to retire for the night. Beryl and her young companions sat talking beside the dying fire. They finished the last bottle of Old John spiced rum as they talked of their family history. Steven succumbed to the secrecy, agreeing that it needed to be kept quiet, although he did not see why the wall had not been demolished long ago and the bones laid to rest, long before the house was handed over to become the hotel. Even Justyna agreed with that. They could have done that long ago, avoiding any problems with the authorities. Still, it was a done deal now and too late to cast blame.

Steven thanked Justyna for staying, when she could have left ages ago. If Justyna believed in ghosts from the start, she would have left after the first night, she declared, laughing. Beryl asked her why she stayed; she knew it was not just because of her grandson. Justyna was not sure. She said she felt that she belonged here, and for once she had found somewhere she felt at home. Not once had she thought about her ex or her friends. Even if she had not met Steven on the shore that day, she would have asked to stay. She reached out, taking his hand, glad that she did meet him.

"You are the first girl I have met who is not after his money," Beryl said. "Most of his tarts were fake — plastic — in brains and body." She laughed.

"Gran, I think you're drunk," he said.

"Who cares? I think I am old enough to say what I think."

Justyna laughed with her, saying that she thought at any age she would have said what she thought.

"You and me both, I think, young lady. Besides, you will make a good lady of the manor. If you decide to take his offer."

The confused look on Justyna's face showed she did not follow what Beryl was saying. She looked across at Steven who was staring at his grandmother, shaking his head again.

"Good grief, you never let it go, do you? Always jumping in, thinking you know everything."

"I know you; you're head over heels in love with the girl. Wild horses would be unable to drag you into The Chine. Yet for Justyna, you happily did," Beryl snickered.

"I wouldn't say happily, Gran."

"You're in love with me," Justyna mocked.

"Don't you start taking her side. I feel I have had enough turmoil tonight, thanks."

With that they decided to call it a night. They walked Beryl to her room on the first floor, then headed to their own room. Steven opened the door, letting Justyna enter.

"So, you love me, then," she teased.

"Right, that's it, you're in trouble now."

He pushed her gently into the room, slamming the door behind him. Then he grabbed her hands, pulling her onto the bed. Down the corridor, in her room, Beryl heard the shrieks of laughter and playful shouting filter through the building. She smiled, happy that her grandson had found a genuine, young lady. A strong-willed, young girl, like herself all those years ago; someone to carry the family name forward and even produce a line of heirs. The thought was replaced as she remembered the trial that awaited them.

In his room, Father Liam was making a phone call. Sat on his bed, he waited for the call to be answered. It rang for a short while before the person answered.

"Martin, it is Liam. Be ready. We will meet you at the west end of the hotel."

That was all he needed to say. Then he knelt, his hands clasped together, and he began to pray.

The Chine remained in darkness that night. No wildlife ventured into the grounds. The animals that foraged along the woods beside the garden boundary, stopped short of the fence, slowly backing away and scurrying back into the safety of the woods.

Inside The Chine, a hallucinatory figure stared out across the grounds, as it drifted through the hotel. Its chilling, whispering, laughing voice echoed through the empty building.

"Come, priest, as before. Your prayers will not help you here."

CHAPTER 10

Martin Cupps was good man. All his life he had tried to do the right thing. He knew his place and was well respected amongst his friends and neighbours. He, like his father and his grandfather, had been church folk since the parish was formed, though not many people knew what sort of connection they had with the church. For the men of the Cupps family were all secular priests, under the governance of a prelate of the Catholic church.

Martin's bloodline had all had careers in technical and agricultural fields, as well as the Catholic spirituality understandings. A lot of wealth was tied up in the Studland estate. It was an exceptional location and one that the church was determined to keep free from accusations of a past misdemeanour. So, to keep the secret safe, the Cupps family were to, as agreed by the Ballard-Young family, maintain the grounds and the estate of The Chine. Nothing was to be excavated, built upon or redesigned without prior agreement, as The Chine was only a leasehold property. Martin and his family had kept the property under their watchful eye for generations.

His whole family knew the story of the slaves and the reason for the haunting. Because of his family's connection to the church, they were sworn to protect the church's name and to uphold the honour of what they stood for. Hence, they were destined to take the jobs that would keep the Ballard's and the Catholic church's secrets. Just that.

When he met Justyna, he wanted to let her know what she was letting herself in for. Various recent events at The Chine had given him cause to worry. He even discussed the hiring of her with Greensmith. He expressed his concerns about bringing a young lady in to look after the hotel over the winter, only to be told that as he was not willing to do so himself, then the hotel had no choice but to hire a permanent caretaker. It seemed that the owner of the hotel wanted the hotel to be protected correctly during its closure.

Martin was sure Justyna would be fine, if she just kept to her room at night. The way she downed her Old John when she first arrived, showed that she was obviously a drinker. Perhaps, then, she would be oblivious. Well, that was what he thought at first.

When he saw her on the beach with Steven, things were taking a turn for the worse. He watched the hotel, as the priest, too, asked him. Father Liam wanted to know what was happening and if the young heir had returned to the hotel. They both knew that should he cross the threshold of The Chine, Nathaniel Ballard would be outraged that the family, who he felt had abandoned him in his hours of need, had dared to enter his home.

Martin was not sure if the ghost of Nathaniel knew The Chine was now a hotel, only for Father Liam to inform him that whatever demon now had hold of his soul, would be aware of what The Chine was. The fact that The Chine was now a hotel had nothing to do with the hauntings — The Chine was just a vessel for evil. The demon had taken a weak man's soul and owned it, purely for its evil purpose.

So Martin watched, and he reported what he saw. He was soon seeing and hearing things that caused concerns for the family. He saw the slaves running around the garden, and he heard the laughter and shrieking. He also heard the piano music from the first night Justyna stayed. He was happy to see she was not fazed by any of it, oblivious to what was happening. Until that early morning when she was in the garden, searching for something. Martin saw Steven arrive. Although he was hidden too far away to hear what they were saying, it was clear she had seen something that bothered her. She was jumpy and skittish. It was then, when she invited Steven into The Chine, that he should have prevented that from happening. This was when he heard, for the first time, the might of the demon's rage. It was terrifying for him, hiding at the edge of the woods. How it must have been for the two youngsters inside The Chine must have been so much worse.

He stalked The Chine from the edge of the woods, moving through the trees, trying to get a better look. Only when he saw the two running to the boy's Land Rover, did he leave to inform the priest.

Father Liam was calm and relaxed as he ever was. Martin arrived at the priest's cottage, nervously revealing all that he had seen: the screaming, and the dark shadows flickering past the lit windows; even how the girl had been searching around the garden in the morning snow, looking for something or someone. Again, he told the priest as he did The Chine manager: it was a mistake putting a young girl in danger this way. The priest informed him that everything had played out the way it was expected to. The girl inviting the heir to the home had brought the demon to light again.

"What do you mean, again? You know this how?"

"As I said, Martin, everything has happened as we imagined."

Martin was not sure what he meant, although he knew what the priest was, and he knew of his past. So he guessed he had somehow crossed paths with the demon. He knew better than to push for further information.

"Thank you, Martin. Your family, and you, have been an immense help to the church. We appreciate your help. Now go home. I will call on you when the time is right. We have one more job to ask of you."

Father Liam placed his hand gently on the small of Martin's back as he spoke. His voice was low and calming, and he smiled at his companion.

Before he knew it, Martin was outside the small cottage, being guided down the garden path. He walked back along the small track which ran across the Purbeck hills. He was able to see the rooftop of The Chine in the distance, hiding beneath the pines. In the falling snow of winter, with the beautiful backdrop of Poole harbour, it looked beautiful. A postcard moment, or a scene from an old biscuit tin. Yet the true horror of The Chine dismissed any real feeling of beauty. Martin drove home, watching The Chine fade away in his mirror as he followed the snow-covered track, as he had done many times before. Inside his heart, he knew his job was done, and he would no longer be needed at The Chine. He could have a holiday — even retire. His bank balance was healthy, as the church had provided his family with a decent wage over the years. When the priest had finished with him, he might be able to rest.

CHAPTER 11

Beryl Ballard was up early most days. Today was a little different. She lay in her bed, thinking. It was going to be a day of days, as her grandson, and his fresh interest, were going to be challenged like nothing before. Her feelings that they would remain safe, even knowing that her friend, the priest, was also going along, held little comfort for her. She knew that Father Liam was hiding something — holding something back. He had been a friend since they were children, even when he left to follow his *persona Christi*. They still wrote to each other often. No, something was wrong. His confidence was, as ever, calm and factual, yet his eyes gave away his nervousness.

Beryl knew what his role had been in the church's order. That was his business, and it made no difference to their friendship. She never questioned him about it, nor did she doubt his beliefs. This morning, when she had the chance, she would ask him what he was hiding — why he was hiding something that she felt endangered Steven and Justyna.

Rothman had set the table for breakfast in the dining room. The room seemed too large for the total number of guests this morning. The large, deep-oak table seemed empty. Rothman set the places around the centre of the table, hoping that keeping the group together would relax them from what was going to be a traumatic day.

Rothman checked his watch, then looked across at the grandfather clock, confirming the time. He wondered why his mistress was not up and about. He shrugged his shoulders as he continued his task.

Steven and Justyna were the first to sit down. Justyna poured them both coffees, complimenting Rothman.

"This is nice, thank you. Though you need not have bothered on our account," she said.

"It was not on your account, miss. This is a normal routine for me at the house," he answered.

Steven looked across at him, shaking his head, expressing his contempt at Rothman's remark. Realizing he had been a little rude, he apologized to Justyna.

"Sorry, Justyna, I feel a little worried about you all. I apologize, and of course I need to bother. You are brave, young lady, as you are, Steven. It is the least I can do for you all."

Steven nodded his appreciation towards the butler, a little shocked that he showed a polite side to him. Father Liam joined them at the table, accepting a coffee from Justyna as he joined them, taking his seat opposite the couple.

Within minutes, Beryl Ballard was sitting alongside her old friend. Nobody ate; they all just took coffee. The table remained quiet as they all drank. Beryl broke the silence first, feeling somebody needed to say something.

"I take it from the reserved conversation of us all that we all feel a little on edge."

"Perhaps I could say a brief prayer — calm our nerves a little," Father Liam added.

"I'd keep that for The Chine, Father. Better there than here, I think," Justyna replied.

"Bless the coffee or something," Steven added.

"If you're as funny as this when we are in the hotel, then I think we will be safe," Justyna said.

That was all it took to get them all talking, as they discussed the plan for the return to The Chine. The priest decided that the sooner they began setting off, the quicker they would be back. Beryl cautioned him about acting like it was just a trip to the shops. It was nothing to brush aside and not to be taken lightly. Father Liam, again in his deep, calm voice, assured his old friend that he had no intention of taking the day lightly.

"I am more than positive that the day will be nothing short of challenging. In fact, I am sure that we are underestimating your late, departed relative. He will wait for us — of this I am sure."

"Well, if we are going to go, can we just go now, as I have no desire to sit here listening to how bad this fellow is, or how he is waiting for us," Justyna replied.

Steven rose, taking Justyna's hand and helping her up, suggesting they get what they need for the journey ahead.

"Gloves, if you have them, and scarves, too, and a warm undercoat. Trust me, you will need it all," Father Liam informed the two.

As soon as the young pair had left, Beryl turned to her friend. She held nothing back, not expressing any anger or malice. She implied she knew he was holding something back. He had something to hide from them — from her.

"You miss nothing, do you? Even after all this time, you seem to think that you are smarter than most."

"Liam, we both know each other well. I doubt you would ask anything less if it was I who was lying to you."

"Lying. No, never. Something is wrong here at The Chine. Apart from the obvious."

"Even more reason to confide in me, Liam. We have too much to lose, should we choose to hide things now. What is it that concerns you?"

"This is not Nathaniel we are dealing with now. You know that. His ghost may inhabit The Chine. This we can agree upon. Yet we lost his soul long ago. Demons prey upon people like Nathaniel. Their love of taking tormented souls and turning them to do their bidding is something we in the church have documented."

"Yes, I know this. What is it that worries you? I am sure you have faced similar in your time, Liam."

"This demon calls to me when I am praying. I hear him mocking me. In my mind, I hear him laughing at me, telling me of my failures. We have crossed paths before. He knows who I am and what I am about to do."

Father Liam stood and walked across to the large bay window, looking out across the rear of the estate. The thick, pink, snow clouds covered the sky. He turned back to Beryl Ballard-Young, holding his arms out at his side, as if he had already given up. Beryl stood up, walking over to him, taking his hands in hers.

"Liam, what is it you want to say? No secrets now, please."

Liam told Beryl the entire story of Abaddon, the demon he had failed to exorcise, and how the evil being had promised they would meet again. He explained that the church believed the demon had somehow known the connection between The Chine and himself and how the conclave had agreed that, in time, he must face the demon again. They believed The Chine would somehow show its dark secrets, as the demon wanted to boast of its powers. The slaves were linked to the demon. Father Liam explained that Abaddon was the keeper of the slaves of hell. Yet he always thought he was a better being than the other angels, even stronger than Satan. Skilled in war, destruction and strategy, Abaddon liked to play deadly games, where he tried to show how strong he was.

"I think he has attached himself to Nathaniel and found a connection to me. He wants to mock me, ridicule my belief. As he beat me before, now he wants to destroy my faith and all who stand with me."

"Liam. Are you sure? That was a long time ago. You were young and naïve, and he played on it."

"I knew what I was doing. Even then, he knew of my past. He knew who you were, Beryl. And he mentioned you by name. He wants to show how strong he is; not to us — to his fellow dark angels. I am sure of it."

"Yes. He may want all that. Though this is your home, Liam, this is your parish. You have come so far now. Back then you were young. Your skills are so much more toned now. Your faith is stronger."

Father Liam turned to look back out of the window. He never doubted himself against Abaddon. It was just the fact that the demon may leave Nathaniel and attach itself to another.

"'Know that I am with you and will keep you wherever you go and will bring you back to this land; for I will not leave you until I have done what I have promised you.'"

"Genesis, Liam. I do not understand. Well, I know Genesis and the verse, but what are you looking for in that script?"

"'But woe to the earth and the sea, for the devil has come down to you,'" the priest replied.

"You can do this, Liam. The church believed in you; they saw something in you. That was why they sent you away to Rome at such an early age."

"Yes, I know. The sacred congregation of St Benedict taught me well. Beryl, the demon told me his name. It is almost unheard of for a demon to do such a thing. He wanted to tell me. The woman was nothing to him."

"He wanted to break your faith. If he knew you were a chosen one, as they say."

"No. For a demon to reveal his name, it means he is weak. He has already lost the battle. Abaddon wanted to show me how strong he was, as if he was better than me. Better than Legion himself."

"Liam. You are a great priest; your heart and soul belong to God. Nothing is stronger than your own doctrine."

He knew she was right, although he felt a right to look scared. Why should not he be?

"Better you feel this now than in that devilish place, Liam."

Once more, Beryl was correct. His faltering at The Chine would show Abaddon he was indeed wary of facing him. No, he must believe in all they had taught him. Every true demonic possession he had attended since he lost to Abaddon, he had triumphed. It mattered not that this demon taunted him. It was to be expected.

"Thank you, my dear friend. I will miss you so very much. I will miss this old house and the warm welcome I always receive."

"Yes, that and the free booze and dinners, too, I expect," Beryl replied.

He squeezed Beryl's hands. She was always a comfort to him. Those days, long ago when he was starting out, her letters were always a comfort and so supportive.

"I know, thank you. Have no fears about Steven and Justyna. I will keep them safe. The role they will play will not be easy, though I expect it will be something that they will never forget."

"As long as you do what we need and return to us safe, all of you."

She suggested they keep the knowledge of the demon between themselves, as it was no point worrying his younger companions.

"Have you spoken to Martin? Is he aware you are going to enter the Chine today?" Beryl asked him.

"I have. He will wait for us at The Chine."

He looked around the room, taking it all in once more. He had memories of good times here. There was always a welcome reception whenever he called by. Now he wished he had called more often.

"I will miss this old house. Not as much as I will miss you, Beryl. I wish we had spent more time together. Still, we both ended up where we belong."

"We were both on different paths, Liam. I could not wish for a better friend than you. Your devotion to the family was far more than the church or my family could expect. I hope it was because of me."

He laughed, knowing that it was. Again, he took her hands, turned them over and kissed them both.

"As a priest, I can only say that I love you as a dear friend and as part of my parish. But a final, long hug would be nice."

They embraced like long-lost lovers, both knowing that this was their last meeting. Beryl kissed him on the cheek. Then they set off to find the rest of the household.

It was an hour later when the three were ready to leave the house. Outside the snow was now falling thick. It was settling as the winds had dropped. Yet the wintry morning temperature was falling fast. Beryl and Rothman both hugged the party as they left the safety of the house. Beryl kissed Justyna on both cheeks, promising that she would see her soon. She whispered into Justyna's ear, telling her she felt happy that her grandson had found a woman worthy of the family name.

Both stood on the steps of the front of the house, watching them walk out into what looked like an enormous white canvas. They sat Gypsy behind the old lady. She barked after her master, sensing the nervousness of the situation. Only when the three became small dots on the white landscape did they enter back into the house, closing the big oak doors behind them. Gypsy took a seat at the base of the stairs, where she would wait for her master to return once more. Her whimpering was low, long and justified, as even she knew that things were not normal.

"What do you think?" Beryl asked, a single tear cascading down her cold cheek.

"Together they will be fine. If they should get separated inside that godforsaken building, I do not know."

Rothman put his arm around her shoulder as he guided her back towards the warm fire. All they could do now was wait.

It took the three of them about an hour, trudging through the snow. Justyna was full of questions. Steven, although scared, with questions of his own, just concentrated on keeping footing as he walked along in the snow. They crossed the fields rather than follow the road, trying to avoid any nosey neighbours who may be active.

Steven fell over as they pushed him to the outside of the trio. Justyna linked arms with the priest. They both laughed in despair at Steven each time he slipped. Father Liam tried to comfort the now cursing young man by saying that it was best to avoid any unnecessary conversations and just get to The Chine as fast as possible.

"Well, that isn't working, is it?" Justyna laughed, as Steven fell again.

Father Liam helped him to his feet, telling him he said to dress appropriate for the conditions, including footwear

Justyna aked him what they should expect. What should they do if they meet the ghosts? The priests laughed at her.

"Oh, you will meet them, that is for sure, my dear. Though how they appear and what they have in mind is anyone's guess."

"Great," Steven said. "So you do not know what to expect, either. Are you sure you have done this before?" he mocked.

"Ah, ye of little faith. I know they may lie to you — play tricks. Imitate your friends' voices, pleading with you to help them. Even pull on your heart strings. Just believe nothing you hear and disregard anything they may say to you. It will be a lie, all of it."

They reached the grounds of The Chine, where they followed the edge of the pines along to the rear of the hotel, opposite the kitchens. Martin was waiting for them, sheltering just inside the woods, sat upon a large backpack.

"Martin, what are you doing here?" Justyna said, shocked.

"It's a long story, better explained when we're finished here," Martin replied.

"Is there no end to the mystery of this place? I feel like I was being used."

"Not at all, my dear. It was just that we needed to monitor The Chine, and you," Father Liam added.

"I am so sorry. We never thought that you would be in any danger. If I could have warned you, I would have done. I wanted to, but…"

They cut him off from pleading his innocence, as the priest once more remarked that this was not the time. Work needed to be done, and they didn't have the time for this discussion.

It was not long before they had made their way around the edge of the tree line, around to the rear of the hotel.

"The lights are on upstairs. They were off a moment ago," Martin told them.

As soon as he had informed them of that, the lights went out once more.

"Just the spirits showing their energy, I guess," Steven replied.

"Perhaps. We need to get to that underground storeroom undetected," Father Liam told them, as they all followed him across the snow-covered lawns.

The cold was biting, and Justyna took Steven's gloved hand, as she felt nervous. They bunched together, all of them, as they tried to keep the bitter wind out of their faces —that and they felt safer huddled close.

Soon they were all on the stone stairs of the bunker, pushing back the snow with their boots, trying to prevent anyone from slipping on the concrete steps. The wind seemed more intense from the sheltered drop of the bunker's steps, as it howled across the top of the steps. Steven held up his torch so Martin could take a lamp from his backpack. He turned it on, illuminating the whole stairwell, then fetched three more similar lamps from his pack, passing them around.

"I thought it would be best if we all had a lamp. If we're going in there, we need to have light," he quipped. Then he took an old set of keys from a small purse, passing them to the priest. "I had these remade with strong steel castings. No point in getting this far and find the old keys were no good."

The priest unlocked the padlocks. They were stiff, and it took a little bit of effort to release the locks. He passed the locks to Martin, telling him to place them somewhere safe in the pack.

"Well, here we are, ready to release these poor souls back to whatever god it is they believed in. I cannot promise it will be a pleasant sight. It is something that we need to do if we are to stand a chance inside The Chine," he told them all.

"Let's just get inside. It's bloody freezing out here," Steven added.

With that said, Father Liam unbolted the door, and he and Martin struggled as they tried to pull the doors open. The smell of dust and dampness filled their senses. As the doors gave, they all entered one by one. Each held up their lamps as they did so, filling the small room with light. It was damp and very musky. The freezing air flowing down the staircase enhanced the smell of the room.

"God, it stinks. What is that smell? It is like an old, rotten apple barn," Steven said.

Father Liam held up his lamp, illuminating the damp brickwork of the wall. They all froze, transfixed by the sight of the wall. Huddled together, they felt uncomfortable with where they were.

"Is that where they are, then? On the other side of this wall?" Justyna asked.

"It is where they were, my dear," the priest replied.

"Yes, I mean that. Is that where they were? They are not there now, are they?" she asked.

"No, of course not, but they are here, on these grounds."

"I know. I saw one of them," Justyna told him.

"Well, they will remain here until I have released them. We need to pass them over to God. Absolve them of their punishment."

Steven stood just behind the other three. His arm was outstretched, holding his lamp above their heads, hoping to shed more light onto the bricked wall. He felt uneasy in the dark and cold room. He was still unsure of what they were there to do. The small, black hand that rested on his shoulder comforted him for a split second, before he realized it was not comforting, as the reason for the coldness of his shoulder dawned on him. He turned his head, keeping his gaze on the small hand resting on his shoulder. His gaze turned to the small, black face looking at him —a transparent face, with a big grin. He was not sure if he dropped his lamp and screamed before the sound of children's laughter filled the room, or after. He lurched forward into his colleagues, as they all crashed against the wall. Justyna screamed as they all dropped their lamps, plunging the room into darkness. Father Liam tried to calm them down as he regained his lamp. He turned it back on, holding it up, as the others got to their feet.

"Son, get a hold of yourself. If I get a heart attack, you are on your own, you know."

"For fuck's sake, Steven, what on earth are you trying to do?" Justyna added.

Steven brushed himself down and looked all around the room, looking for the boy.

"I saw a boy. In fact, he was standing right behind me; his hand was on my bloody shoulder. I mean, for crying aloud. What do you expect me to say or do? Introduce myself and ask him to join us?"

"Who did you see? Was it the slave?" Father Liam asked.

"Are you sure you saw a boy? It was just, you know, in your head. It is creepy here," Justyna said.

"How do I know who it was? I guess he could be. You heard the laughing. Or was that in my head? That was kids laughing, and he was right behind me, just looking at me," Steven replied.

"Then they know we are here and why we are here. Which means, I am afraid to say, Nathanial knows we are here, too," Father Liam informed them both.

"If it is still him, I think whatever he once was, has long been taken over by the demon you mentioned Justyna added, taking Steven's hand.

Father Liam thought about letting them know he had crossed the demon long ago. The demon was waiting for him to face him once more. This was going to be his last exorcism; one that would be far more dangerous that anything he had faced. Perhaps if they knew, they would not be so sure about being at The Chine. So he chose to keep it to himself. Better they did not know too much about what was to come.

A huge, distant roar broke his thoughts as the angry sound echoed across the gardens, filtering down the stone steps into the cellar. As one, they all turned to look towards the door. Justyna gripped Steven's hand tighter, feeling on edge. Although she understood what was going on, she never felt the fear until now. It was no joke. It was like some terrible movie she had seen in the past. This was real, and for the first time, she felt scared. More so, as she had been sleeping in The Chine. Anything could have happened to her.

"I am so glad that my friend never came to stay here. If anything had happened to her, well, I would never forgive myself."

Martin looked back at her, asking her if she had invited her friend to stay, only to find out that she had indeed asked her. But Justyna mentioned that her friend was a little indecisive and that didn't always do what she said she would. Justyna said she was glad she was not here, with all this going on. It was enough for her to take it all in. To have to explain it to somebody else was too much.

"Imagine if she was here, looking for me," she said with concern.

"Do you think she would have rung and told you if she was coming?" Steven replied.

Father Liam told them to be quiet and to concentrate on the task at hand. He ran his hands across the icy wall in front of them. The chilling laughing they had heard convinced him they were in the right location. The room was now cold, more than just down to the bitter conditions.

"Come on, lend me a hand. We need to get behind this wall," the priest whispered.

Martin took two large screwdrivers from his coat, passing one to the priest. Then they scraped away at the cement between the brickwork. Steven held the lamp up, watching them work, while Justyna kept looking behind her. Not sure what she was looking for, she just felt that they were not alone. In the back of their half of the room, in the darkness of the corners of the room, the blackness seemed to shimmer and move. Not wanting to sound scared, she kept quiet while the two men picked apart the cement.

"What is it? What are you looking at?" Steven asked her.

"Nothing. It's just that, well, I think something, or someone, is with us, watching."

"What, where?" he asked her, in a whispered voice.

"Promise not to scream again," she joked.

"Is it the boy again, or worse?"

"Look, in the corner over there. Something is there."

"Yes, it has been here since we first came in the door. Ignore it. No harm will come from him," the priest answered.

"You knew it was here? And what, waiting for you or us to come?" Steven asked.

He was confused and angry. Did the priest know what was in store, or was this some expected church knowledge? Either way, he felt the priest was holding something back from Justyna and himself. He wanted to challenge him, but as he was about to say something, the two other men began pulling the brickwork apart. Bricks fell to the floor around the men's feet, each sending a hollow-like echoing sound across the closed half of the room. As they pulled brick after brick away, the shimmering image from the corner of the room began swirling around the room. Justyna held onto Steven, hugging him tight as Steven held his lamp up, trying to follow the eerie presence as it circled them, faster and faster.

Then the priest stepped away from the wall, pulling Martin away with him. He held his lamp up, illuminating the large hole they had now created. The circulating shadow disappeared into the other side of the room. None of the party spoke as, one by one, they began peering into the opposite room.

Light filtered into the now open half of the room, the slight swinging of the held-up lamps causing the image from the other side to fade in and out of the light and then back into the shadows. Father Liam leant forward and rested his own lamp on the floor, and the room filled with light. After he surveyed the room, he turned back to the others, inviting them to look inside. Martin, being by his side, was the first to peer inside. Shaking his head from side to side, he said nothing. He then invited the two youngsters to see for themselves. Father Liam halted them first, warning them it may not be pleasing to see.

Justyna and Steven walked forward to the gap, stepping over the heap of bricks on the floor. Justyna held her hand up to her mouth as she took in what the room revealed. A circle of preserved skeletons were sitting upon the floor, bones intact, as if they were plastic models or props, placed there for a movie set. Steven looked shocked, and he stepped into the room.

"My ancestors did this?" he questioned the priest.

"Son, it was a long time ago, and you are about to set things right. Please, do not feel this was anything more than the act of one crazy man. This was not your family's doing."

The priest stepped inside, joining him. Picking his lamp up, he surveyed the room. He held his lamp up, moving it above the heads of the seated occupants.

"Count them, count them. One is missing," Justyna said, from the other side of the room.

"Yes, I dare to say that the apparition with us is, in fact, the boy, Emanuel."

"You think so? He is not sat with them?" she asked.

"Where is his skeleton? He never escaped? The book we read was wrong," Steven added, sounding confused.

"Well, we believe he was, in fact, much more than just a slave. From what we know, he was an extraordinarily strong *nganga*. A witch doctor, as you would call it today."

"But this was a boy. He could not be a *nganga*, or whatever it was you called him," Steven replied.

Father Liam walked to where the circle contained a small gap, where the chain of held hands had broken. He knelt in the gap and began rubbing his hands across the dirty floor. He found a necklace, made up of small, sharp teeth. They tied long, faded feathers to the string trailing the teeth. The string fell apart as he held it up to the light. He caught the quill of one feather, twisting it in his fingers. The feathers, over time, had become matted together, caked in dust and dirt. They had long since lost any true beauty.

"Made from a rat or mouse. The feathers are from a chicken or a pheasant. A typical — what the Africans call — a *Nkisi* style of dress. The boy would have been sitting here. He would have cast his spiritual knowledge at this location. He would have summoned the demon that took over Nathanial, here, to show the demon had no power over his faith."

"You are kidding! A boy did that? All this is because of a boy?" Justyna asked

"Wait a minute. The book said he was a Vodoun god-like thing," Steven replied.

"It is all linked. Voodoo, as you know it, is an African-based belief. The Iwa and the Vodoun. This Iwa may be on his third or fourth cycle; you know — born again. We know children have such powers in Africa," Martin added.

"The different belief in the African faith would conflict the demon. Although it has no control over the young slaves, it would still hold the slaves on the grounds."

"Yes, as Martin says, the boy did this. He was powerful indeed, yet even with his own power, still unable to leave. This was why you saw them."

Steven took in the circle's image of skeletons. He felt sorry for what had happened. For a long time, he had been against the way his family had inherited their wealth. Now, the thought that he was helping to correct

197

a small part of it made him feel a little better. He felt the hand squeezing his shoulder, comforting him in his thoughts. He was about to ask Father Liam what the next step was. However, as he looked over to the priest, he noticed that Martin and Justyna were standing together, looking at him. No, they were looking past him. It was only then that he thought, that if they were all stood in front of him, whose hand was squeezing his shoulder? He was desperate to look, yet terrified because he knew who it was.

With a slow turn of his head, the boy, Emanuel, met him. Martin and Justyna stepped back behind Father Liam, both hoping for intervention. Father Liam took a step towards the now frozen Steven, only for Emanuel to hold his hand up to halt the priest. The ghostly image of the boy turned his palm down, then moved his hand across to the right in a swinging arc, as his other hand kept hold of Steven's shoulder. Emanuel turned his gaze back to Steven, nodding his ghostly head towards the circle, wanting Steven to follow. It was an image that left him terrified, and he remained rooted to the spot. There, sat on the floor, in the same place as the skeletons were, now sat the figures of the entombed slaves. They were each sitting as they were when Nathanial Ballard had left them so many years ago.

Emanuel dropped his hand from Steven's shoulder and walked up to the others, studying them each. He stopped in front of Father Liam, smiled, then bowed his head and took his place in the circle. As they all joined hands, they once more lowered their heads. Then the chanting began, as it did many years ago.

Martin took it upon himself to explain that now was the time for the release of the Haitian's souls. They were to keep silent, while Liam did his work. Father Liam ushered them away as he moved around the circle, taking his place behind the young boy, Emanuel. As the priest held his hands out across the chanting group, he voiced his sanctum, beginning the slaves' release from the tomb that had a grip on their discomfort —a release that would set their spirits free to return home to their own lands.

The priest was aware of how the demon inside The Chine would react, knowing that God's work was being carried out nearby. It would now look for them, waiting for them to enter The Chine. It was going to be a hard struggle; more for his companions than himself. However, the less they were aware of what they were about to face, the better.

He continued with his sermon. His companions had now moved back into the previous half of the room. The screeching began emitting from The Chine and carried across the wintery storm winds, the sound echoing over the gardens. The snowstorm was thick and constant now, and it was hard to make out any structures across the grounds. Steven and Justyna huddled together at the bottom of the steps. Shivers ripped through them both. They were cold and frightened. They knew now that it was very real. There was no going back now, although

Justyna felt that there was far worse to face. It was more frightening than any horror they had seen so far. It was a long way to being over for them all —an exceptionally long way.

"I am so glad that I never asked Edyta to come and visit, like I had planned to," Justyna whispered.

It was then that Martin realized that the unknown car was her friend's car. It was not a local car. He knew all the vehicles in the area, along with who owned them. No tourist would brave the harsh winter weather unless they were here to visit. He hoped that he was wrong — he prayed he was wrong. However, the trenches in the deep snow leading away from the car to The Chine, were a clear sign that somebody had made their way to the grounds. It was better to say nothing to Justyna or the priest. They all had enough to concern themselves with already. There was no point in adding fuel to the fire.

CHAPTER 12

The priest was done with his work and was content with how it had gone. They were all soon heading across the garden towards the front of the hotel. All around them the wind howled, and the icy chill bit into any bare skin on show. They held onto each other as they plodded across the deep snow that had now accumulated and was driven into every corner of the grounds by the fierce winds. With every step, the winds were trying to force them back, as it whipped the surrounding snow into a frenzy. It was almost blinding them, as they all tried to keep upright, heading forwards to the entrance of the building.

Father Liam led the way, struggling to keep the image of the hotel in his sights. He made his way, forcing one step after another, trying to shield the others behind him. The Chine. Then, nothing. No snow, no more forceful winds, nothing — just intense cold.

"Jesus Christ, what is happening? Are we in the eyes of a tornado or something?" Steven asked, apologizing for the religious metaphor.

"It's Nathanial's demon — playing games — isn't it?" Justyna asked.

The priest stamped his feet on the hard, icy top of the covered entrance as he brushed the snow from his jacket. He removed his gloves, blowing warm air into his cupped hands. He knew the demon was waiting for them, along with whatever else was hiding within The Chine.

"Listen, whatever happens, try to keep together. Do not wander off on your own now. Once we set foot inside this building, nothing you see will be real. Believe nothing you see or hear."

"The demon is real, though — you said he was real," Steven said.

Justyna elbowed him, shaking her head, trying to get him to stop talking and making things worse.

The priest pushed open the large door, asked if they were ready, then he stepped inside The Chine.

"What did you hit me for? I was just checking to see if this demon was real. No need to hit me," Steven complained.

"It is no time to get into a discussion about stupid things like that with Father Liam, when we are on the doorstep, about to see the bloody demon. And of course the demon is real."

They were all stood in The Chine's lobby, the bare light from outside penetrating no further than a few feet. They lit the lanterns, shedding light into the darkness. The door slammed behind them, yet none of them turned to find a cause. As they fanned out along the entrance, they each held up their lanterns. It offered little to them, only throwing up shadows across the walls.

Justyna advised Father Liam that they should check the reception office out first and try the lights. With that, they followed the priest around the desk to the manager's office. Martin and Steven brought up the rear, each walking backwards, lanterns held outstretched and high, checking every corner and hallway as they stepped backwards, following the other two. They both tried to squeeze through the office door, neither wanting to give way.

Justyna tried all the light switches. Yet nothing seemed to work. The Chine remained in darkness. The sound of the wind was haunting in its passage as it swept through the building.

"It looks like we are going to be exploring in the dark, then," Martin told them.

"Of course, I never said it was going to be easy. Just remember what I said. Stick together."

"Where do we start? It is a big hotel," Steven asked the priest.

"I think Nathanial will be somewhere he knows — a place that was his. So, what was once his room? I am not sure; this differs from an exorcism. There is no host — no living one, anyway."

As they made their way back into the lobby area, the sound of laughing began again —faint at first, then it was all around them. It encircled them before it trailed away into the lounge area of the hotel. Justyna informed them that this was the room that led out into the rear gardens.

"The room that has the piano, which plays in the night," Martin said.

Justyna turned to look across at him, his face glowing with an orange tint, reflective from his lantern.

He turned to meet her stare. "I have heard it, once or twice, in the night."

She wanted to know when, as she was sure she had never heard it before. Was it while she had been staying there, or was this something new that he had heard?

"It is nothing new to me," he replied.

Huddled together, they made their way down the few steps towards the middle of the room, three or four feet away from the piano.

"I am sure I had a dream about listening to someone play that. It was not a dream, then," Justyna said.

"Did you dream about her, too?" Steven asked, pointing behind her.

"Who, about who?" she replied.

Across the room, next to the fire, the smoky, fading image of Wyn, the housekeeper, was levitating. Arms folded, she faded in and out of focus as she approached the group.

Justyna spoke to Father Liam, informing him it was she who helped them escape The Chine earlier. As the priest stepped forward to challenge the ghostly apparition, Wyn swooped forward, her image now a haunting vision of a disfigured, rotting face. She was dressed in tattered rags which were hanging from her ghostly body. One side of her face was smashed beyond recognition, her eye socket hollow and cracked. Her voice was not the one that had calmed Justyna. Now it was high-pitched — a scream.

"Do not challenge me, Priest! I need not your protection or retribution."

Her image disappeared, only to reappear behind him, before instantly fading to stand before him.

"This is the image he wishes you to see. It is not one I cherish."

Then, as she backed away, the image of Ms Wyn reformed. She smiled at Justyna as she moved in and amongst the four of them. Then she took her place in front of Father Liam.

"Thank you for freeing the little ones. It pleased them you came to them. They knew you would. But you need to take the young lady away. This is not her ground; she is not safe. He will take her; he will try to take you all."

"It is OK. I am safe with Liam."

The old girl was not listening; she was focused on Steven. It was as if she moved through him, as she examined the now shaking inheritor.

"You had no right to return here, in the master's eyes. You abandoned him when he needed help. Your family felt disgraced, yet you reaped his rewards. He said you should have stayed away. His anger will now power the demon that has him."

"I know of this demon, Abaddon. We have crossed paths before," Father Liam answered.

"Yes, you have, therefore you must be strong, and your faith must be strong. You know he wants you, Father — he needs you. This demon cares not for these others. Up there somewhere, he is waiting for you," Ms Wyn replied.

She turned her head away from the group as the slaves speared, their images flickering in and out. Their ghostly hands reached out to Ms Wyn, pulling at her, whispering to her, warning her. The sound of a deep, booing voice echoed through the hotel, and the children, along with Ms Wyn, were gone.

The four visitors backed away, out of the room, back into the reception lobby. They kept close to the wall, moving around the furniture. Justyna mentioned the portraits — how she took them down, only to find them back on the wall later. Steven expressed his discomfort at this, saying that if he knew, he would have taken her away ages ago. Nor would he have set foot in The Chine. Justyna mocked him for being such a wimp, asking how he expected to talk to her if he was too scared to even come into the hotel.

Father Liam felt that the two of them would need that bond they seemed to have formed, as he was sure that things were going to be far worse than he had first imagined. If the old lady knew Abaddon had met him before, then the demon had the upper hand. Even though he trusted his faith, knowing that if he asked for God's guidance now, he might see it as a lack of belief. For once he smiled to himself, one last time. This would be his finale, to earn his place of peace, and study at the Vatican. It was time to go home.

Martin held his lamp up to study the portraits that Justyna had mentioned. All of them followed suit, examining the haunting portraits.

"Painted at the height of their success, showing them in all their splendour," Steven added. "They appear very strict — almost evil — even back then."

"They did Victorian era portraits in a manner where they never smiled. Back in the day, all portraits from that era were solemn looking," Martin said.

A slow moan began, as they all closed ranks, back to back, to cover all directions. They were unsure where it was coming from, holding their lamps up high above their heads, asking each other if they could see anything.

"It's him, the guy in the portrait — it's coming from him," Martin said.

They all turned to face the wall, lifting and lowering their lanterns to get a better view and shed more light on the wall. Then the face of Leandro Fischer turned to look down at them, his face protruding out of the canvas as it turned, observing them each of them, laughing as he did so. Someone jostled Justyna into the middle of the group to protect her from this spectre. Fischer was ebbing his way out of the frame, growing as he did so. He stepped down on the back of the sofa below the portrait, balancing on the back of the leather seat. He dropped, as if he had a thousand times before, onto the cushion of the sofa, his arms stretched across the top in both directions. He was looking away from them, his gaze facing into the hallway as if he had no interest in the group, drumming his fingers on the leather.

Father Liam was halfway to raising his crucifix to repel the ghost, only for Fischer to shoot forward. His face was a screaming, distorted mess, his deep, matt, black eyes seeming to go on far beyond his head. The tied hair that was clear in the portrait was now a mass of knotted strands. Black veins shot across his pale face.

Fischer flew at Martin, knocking the man clean across the room and into the reception counter. His lamp crashed into the floor, extinguishing the light. Father Liam told Justyna and Steven to stay where they were, and he rushed over to his friend. As Martin got to his feet, he searched for his lantern, desperate to relight it. The priest got to it first and relit it for Martin, asking his friend if he was OK. Martin took the lantern, holding it up to search the area.

"I think I may have some bruises tomorrow, apart from…"

That was all he said before he shot backwards at a frightening speed, as if on a huge, bungee elastic cord, stretched beyond its limit. An invisible laughing force dragged him away, screaming for help, into the darkness behind him, his arms stretched forward, slamming onto the floor, reaching out for his friends. His face seemed pale in the half light from the lantern in his hand, as he tried to keep it from smashing. Then he was gone. The light, like his terrified face, faded away in the dark, the screaming now silent.

Justyna spoke first, her voice hesitant, as she asked Steven what was happening. His answer never came. He looked confused. He stood looking at the priest, hoping for any kind of guidance or reassurance. But the man offered none. He just turned and headed back down the hall. The two stood in shock, looking back towards where Martin had been standing at the reception desk, then back at the priest. They were both helpless —afraid and helpless — as the hotel turned back into darkness. They both turned and pursued Father Liam.

"What the fuck was that? We must help him. The poor man."

"And do what, and to what? We just need to leave. The slaves are free now. We should just knock the place down."

"I do not think that will help him, or us, Steven," Father Liam added.

"Come on, we need to follow him. It does not mean he is dead. Keep the faith. Stay focused, you said," Justyna added.

Steven gripped Justyna's arm, pulling her closer to him. "Keep the faith. With whatever that was, or whoever, it is going to be hard to believe anything ever again."

"That was Nathaniel's sidekick; you know — the captain. The guy from the portrait," she replied.

Father Liam reminded them of what he told them earlier, that this was how the demon wanted them to react. He wanted them to chase shadows and doubt their faith. They had to be stronger. Whatever happened, they had to push through to the end. Nothing they saw was real. These ghosts were just there to make them weak. So, when they met the demon, he would already have the upper hand.

Steven doubted what he heard, even though he knew it was important to believe and have the faith that the priest insisted they have. That something took Martin in the way it did. It was hard not to believe it was not true.

Once again, he pulled Justyna close to him, as he whispered into her ear. "He should have told Martin it was not real. He might still be here then."

Lanterns held high, they walked back down the corridor towards the bar, pausing at the restaurant, where Justyna suggested they might be in the kitchen area or the staff rooms. Father Liam dismissed the idea. He was positive that they needed to head upwards.

"I am sure that Abaddon will wait upstairs, channelling all his power through Nathanial. This, so far, is nothing — just his minions playing a game with us.

"A game. I doubt Martin found it as a game. Do you think he is safe, or even alive?"

"I cannot say, Justyna. Look, you two cannot help me much more than this. If you think you can help Martin, then find him. I can face this demon on my own. It is me he wants, not you two."

"Sounds great to me," Steven added.

"Steven. Do not be a wimp. Are you sure that is the best idea, Liam?"

"Yes, go, but be ready for anything. You have your crucifixes. Just believe in what you are saying and deny them everything."

And with that said, the priest made his way up the stairs to the upper floors, leaving the two youngsters to search for Martin. They were about to check the restaurant when Justyna caught a movement out of the corner of her eye. She grabbed Steven's arm, pulling him back.

"There, look at the corner of the bar. Someone is hiding."

"Where? I cannot see anything. It is just your reflection from the mirror behind the bar."

"No, not there. Look, in the corner by the window, crouched in the corner."

They both took slow steps, matching each other's stride as they entered the bar. And there in the corner, something seemed propped up at the back of the room. They both knew from their last visit to the bar that it had not been in the room before. Justyna held out her lantern, trying to shed light into the corner of the room. As they neared, the dim light revealed a hunched, half-hidden body. Its torso was twisted and disfigured. One leg was outstretched, the foot twisted backwards, the bone of the ankle protruding and shattered. Long dark hair was hiding the face.

"Holy shit, is that a girl? It is not Martin, or is it?"

Before Justyna could answer Steven, the sound of cracking bones filled the room, as the disfigured body raised and turn its head. The sound of bones cracking and snapping together froze the pair to where they stood, as the broken body of Edyta got to her feet.

"Why did you leave me here, Justyna? You were my friend. Why did you do this to me?"

"Edyta, is that you? Oh, my god, what happened to you?"

"Who is it? Is this your friend? No, it cannot be. It is a trick, Justyna."

Edyta's deformed head was twisted halfway around her neck, her bones breaking the skin protruding through her neck. She turned her head round with a sickening snap, her hair floating in the dim light, hiding her face, as she turned to look at Steven, screaming at him in a voice unknown to Justyna.

"Fuck off, you are not welcome here! You and your kin have no right to enter The Chine."

"No, it is her, but it isn't her, if you know what I mean," Justyna whispered. "Edyta, I am so sorry. How did you get here? What has happened to you?" she continued.

She mocked Justyna, mimicking her voice and repeating what she had said. She tried to stand upright, only for the sickening sound of more bones cracking and snapping to be heard once more. Her legs were now twisted out of shape, her ankles almost horizontal to the floor. Yet she still tried to remain upright, as she tried to walk towards the pair. Who was now backtracking away from her? Edyta placed her broken leg forward, the bone splintering as it hit the floor, as she then dragged her other twisted foot along the floor. The sound of the bone splintering was sickening, so much so that Justyna could feel the vomit rising in her stomach.

"How did I get here? You invited me — your best friend. Are you not happy to see me? Shall we have a drink? We all know how much you love a drink. Have a drink, you bitch."

Bottles began flying off the bar, crashing into the walls beside Steven and Justyna. Bottle after bottle bounced off the furniture, ricocheting off the walls. The alcohol, along with broken glass, sprayed over the retreating pair who were trying to keep their balance.

"Edyta, stop! This isn't you, please," she begged.

Again, Edyta imitated Justyna, mocking her further, as she limped and lunged towards the pair, laughing at them.

"Please, Edyta, please Edyta. Look at me, you slut. You did this. Now he wants you. He knows you are here. I want you to feel the pain I felt — you and this shit of an heir."

213

Edyta raised her twisted right arm behind her, to the bar. As she did so, the bar became engulfed in flames, its blue, flickering light fuelled by the spilt alcohol. Its dancing flame raced across the bar, down to the floor and across the floor towards Steven and Justyna, who were now stood amongst the broken glass and spilled alcohol. Before they could react, the room resounded in children's laughter, growing louder. Edyta thrust her head from left to right, twisting it in every direction as she backed away. There, in front of Justyna and Steven, stepping out from the flames as if part of the fire, the evanescent images of the slaves emerged, surrounding the now shrieking Edyta. Steven once more felt a hand pressing on his shoulder. This time, though, he knew it was Emanuel.

"Take out your cross. You must take the cross and free her from this torment."

Steven didn't hesitate; he knew what he had to do. There was no time to doubt. He strode forward and implanted the cross against Edyta's forehead. There was no resistance from the disfigured Edyta. She emitted an ear-splitting shriek, but there was no fight in her. The slaves had encircled her. They had frozen her in their circle, somehow, making her powerless. After a brief time, Edyta dropped to the floor, motionless. The flames died down and disappeared, as did the slaves. Justyna ran across to Steven and to her friend. What was the disfigured, smashed and broken Edyta a moment ago, was now a more recognizable friend.

Steven knelt beside her, feeling her neck. "I am so sorry, but she is gone. No pulse, nothing."

"It was not her, was it? Well, it was, but at the end, it was not her."

"I do not know who it is or was. Whoever it was, I am sad to say she is dead now."

Justyna revealed to him who it was, as tears ran down her cheeks. She squatted down beside the limp carcass of her best friend, taking her hand in her own.

"I am so sorry. You deserved none of this. I am so sorry."

Steven asked why she had never called to say she was going to come, only to be told that that was what Edyta did. She never answered her phone when you called her. Then she just turned up unexpectedly. It was what made her so special.

"Despite this, she was my best friend. Now I have gotten her killed."

"Hey, come on, this is not down to you. Do not think like this. You heard what Liam said to us. If we are not strong, he, or it, will be greater for it."

She knew he was right, but the guilt trip was already rolling. Her best friend was dead. She stood up, walked behind the bar and took the bottle of Old John, taking a tremendous hit from it. She offered it to Steven who followed suit.

"Right, then, let us get whatever is awaiting. We have some help."

"Yes, we do. Sinister help, but at least they are help."

They made their way back to the lounge area where the lights seemed to flicker on and off, shedding light across the reception lobby. The smell of the sweet perfume once again filling the hallway.

"I think we may have more help to come," Justyna said.

Arm in arm, they made their way along the corridor. She noted that the portraits were missing from the wall. She was about to tell Steven what had transpired earlier, when all of a sudden she felt nervous. It was the way the portraits observed her, so she took them down and turned them around to face the wall.

Before she had finished, the melody of the piano began. As they both squinted into the lounge, the wall-mounted lights started glowing, yielding sufficient light across the room. It was like an old, Victorian photo show. An image of the ghostly figure at the piano appeared in and out of focus. Justyna pulled Steven forward as she tiptoed down into the lounge, and within seconds the sound of children running and laughing besieged them. Steven tried to haul Justyna back out of the lounge, pulling at her arm, only for her to traipse forward towards the piano, yanking him along with her.

"Look, it is her — the old lady. We are OK. She means us no harm."

"You do not know that. For all you know, it could be her who transported Martin away."

"No, it is Wynn, the housemaid. It must be her. See, the slaves are with her. It must be her, Steven."

She was right. The translucent image of the old lady was now flanked on both sides of the piano by the young slaves. They were all singing, yet they heard no sound above the melody of the piano. It was a ghostly, odd image, one only to be broken by the roar — a resentful, long growl of displeasure — that filled the room. Without indecision, the two both scurried over to the piano, feeling they would be safe, somehow. Wyn displayed an affectionate smile to them as she stood. Her spectral presence flowing through the dark wood of the piano, she took her place alongside the two fearful youngsters.

"Why have you returned? I cautioned you not to remain," Wynn demanded.

"We had to come back. This must end today," Steven replied.

"The priest knows what calls for to be done. This is not for you to face. Leave now. Nathanial requires no further help from you now."

"I must stay and help him. We both do. Will you help us?" Justyna asked.

"I cannot help you further. I have no power here. This demon has so much sin. He has been lingering, knowing he will come."

"Who, Steven? He knew Steven was coming?"

Wyn moved around them, taking her place behind the slaves, her gliding cloud like spirit waning.

217

"No, the priest. He knew the priest would come back to face him once more. He wants him, and only him. You and your friends mean nothing to him."

The room became chilly —icy cold — as the sudden boom of an echoing voice sounded out, stopping any further conversation.

"*Enough!*" the voice roared.

The slaves surrounded the three figures at the front of the piano, forming a barrier between them and whatever was coming.

"I had warned you before, woman, many times over. Yet you still meddle with these heathen people. Do you never learn your place?"

The voice seemed to reverberate around the room. Justyna looked all around, looking to locate the possessor.

Wyn levitated further out into the room, her transparent image flickering in and out of focus. In an instant, the spectre of Leo confronted her, bellowing out his dismay. Leo noticed Steven and became more enraged. His ghostly figure circled the room at speed, his face fixated on the heir.

"You dare to come here now; you and your woman, and that weak, pitiful man of God. This hag will not protect you."

"Look at you; once a proud man of the sea. Respected and loyal, now just a puppet to the demon of this house," Wyn added.

" *Silence!*" Leo bellowed at her. "Let us show them the real you, shall we? Let them see who they think will save them in all her true glory."

He flew down to the piano, laughing. All in one movement, he was floating up at the high ceiling again, looking down on his handy work. Wyn had now transformed into her skeletal self, as she would look after the past hundred years had eaten away at her: a damaged skull with a great crack in the side, where Nathanial had beaten her so violently. Her once perfect hair, once tied in a neat bun, was now only three or four clumps and strands of long, white hair. Deep, black eye sockets stood out, even in the dim light.

Wyn turned to Justyna, her previous image returning in an instant. Her calming smile once more returned.

"He has no power here, my child. Fear not."

Leo had no chance to reply, as Emanual held his hand out towards him, beckoning to him. "You are a pirate and a murderer. Your time here is done. For what you did, in the name of your god, they have judged you, Leandro Fischer."

Leo swooped down to the young slave, ready to retaliate, only to come to a dead stop, as if frozen in time.

"Your god left you a long time ago, white man. Your friend is no longer anyone close to who you once knew. This Abaddon has no need for you. It has no interest in you. To it, you are nothing; a sheep that did its master's bidding."

Leo protested at this outrageous claim, trying to raise his voice, only for the boy to step forward, examining the now distressed apparition.

"Your so-called god did not warrant your actions, now you will answer to mine."

As he finished his sentence, the room trembled. The remaining slaves encircled Leo, forming a ring around him. A bright light formed above them, as if a split in time was opening. The sound of galloping horses filled the room. Steven put his arm around Justyna, wanting to pull her away from what was about to happen, only for Wyn to say they were safe and they had no reason to be fearful.

"Justyna, come on, we need to get out of here. This is way too fucking weird for me."

"No, wait, I want to see what happens," Justyna replied.

Leo was trying to twist his head to see what was coming, but Emanual had him frozen in mid-air. Then, bursting through the light, the black horses spilled out. Behind them was the massive image of a dark man, black as night itself. He was dressed in a tailcoat, and atop his head was a large top hat, giving him more height. A cigar was hanging from his mouth, releasing large plumes of white smoke that masked his face. He guided his charges around the room before jumping down to face the slave, Emanual.

"Why have you called me, boy? Do you know what this means to demand I come here?"

The deep voice was obvious to where its roots belonged, as was the darkness of his skin. He was an Abu, as was Emanual, though this was Papa Guede, a powerful loa; also known as Baron Criminal to the believers in voodoo and Vodun. He was a much-feared loa spirit, only summoned to offer swift justice, where he would kill any past criminal if necessary.

As he walked around the now silent Leo, his colourful appearance was more transparent. They had edged his long tailcoat in purple trim. His waistcoat was white, and his hat was blood red. He drew on his cigar, filling the area with a disgusting stench. He walked up to the helpless Leo and began shouting obscenities at him, belittling the old captain.

"We know what you have done. We have been waiting for you. Watching. Waiting," he laughed.

Leo tried to protest, only for the Baron to scream at him once more, cursing him, explaining that even the demon Abaddon had no powers to stop them claiming his soul —little that remained.

The ghostly images of the slaves faded away, leaving just Emanual, the Baron and Leo at the front of the piano. The Baron pointed to the far corner of the room, sending the ghostly black horses away. They seemed to fade away then return at full speed, heading straight for Leo, who was then dragged away under the ghostly hoofs and into the open light.

Emanual turned to Steven and Justyna, both who were standing open-mouthed, shocked by what they had just witnessed.

"This is all I can do to help you. We have no power here, other than to our own kin. And to those who harm our children. As a loa, I summoned the Guede. Long ago, we agreed this was the only way to pass in peace. Locked away in that tomb, we have been waiting for release, free from the grip of this demon Abaddon. Your priest gave us this. We can now pass over and rest."

"But what about this demon? Will the priest be able to defeat it? Can you offer no help to us at all?" Steven asked.

"He knows what he must do. For you, just believe in him, and you will succeed."

The boy drifted across the room to Wyn, who took his hand. She smiled at Steven and Justyna. Then they were gone. The room was empty and silent. Darkness once more was their only companion. The smell of cheap cigar smoke filled their nostrils, as the Baron's presence remained.

"Well, I suppose we better go up to find Father Liam," Justyna said.

"Brilliant. I was hoping you would say we should leave. Before it gets weird."

They both made their way back towards the stairs, along the dark corridor. Both were aware that any help they may have had was now gone. Neither mentioned what had happened, yet they were both glad it did.

However, all thoughts of what had happened to Martin were also gone. Justyna stopped outside the bar, looking in where Edyta lay crumpled in the corner. She stepped into the bar, and Steven grabbed her arm, holding her back.

"You cannot help her more. She has gone."

"I know. It is not her I am looking for. If we are going upstairs, I want to make sure I have a drink first."

Justyna knew what she was looking for as she stepped around the bar. After a brief search, she found the bottle of Old John.

"This is the best spiced rum I ever tasted, and I think we're going to need a stiff drink after we beat this shit of a demon."

" OK, well, I will not argue with that. And when this is done, I will take you to the Urban Reef bar where it was made. You can tell them yourself."

They took a quick swig each then climbed the stairs into the darkness above. Steven whispered Father Liam's name with each step. After searching the first floor and discovering nothing, they moved on to the top floor, finding the priest standing at the top of the stairs waiting for them. The freezing air hit them in an instant; a biting cold that caught their breath, tightening their chests.

The priest stood looking down at them as they ascended the stairs. He looked cold as he held out a shivering hand, beckoning them to him.

"He is here, waiting for us. In fact, waiting for me, in there."

He held his lamp up then pointed towards the room at the far end. The brightness that filled the narrow cracks in the doorframe, from the room at the end of the dark corridor, was intense, as if there were a thousand lights behind the door. Yet it barely penetrated the darkness it intruded. It was more of a fluorescence glow, a warning of what may lay on the other side. Somehow, it was tempting you to investigate, even though you knew that whatever was on the other side was not good.

As all three walked forwards to the door, Father Liam once again reminded them to keep the faith —to believe in God's name, no matter what their faith may have been prior to this day.

"Do not believe in anything that whoever on the other side of the door may say. It will want to deceive and confuse you. It will all be a lie. You must not consider or think on what it may reveal to you."

They both nodded in agreement, yet the motion was lost to the priest in the darkness of the corridor. He demanded they answer him.

"Do you understand?" he shouted. "You have to be aware of what we are about to encounter."

"We do, we both do," Steven answered.

"Yes, of course we do," Justyna added.

They began to slowly approach the room. When they were just a few yards away, the laughing started. Its deep laugh echoed around them, sounding off behind them. The cold began to ease away only to be replaced by a warmth that was more uncomfortable than the cold. It was as if someone had opened an oven door; a vast oven door like a kiln. The heat swept over them as they neared the door. Father Liam reached forward to open the door, his hand inches from the handle. Suddenly the door flew open before them, and the laughing stopped.

"Come, face me again, priest. Bring your minions; they will be of no use to you here."

CHAPTER 13

Callum Hopkins had just made a break of forty-five and was about to increase his lead over his friend, Mark, when the lights from a car driving up the driveway of the estate made him look towards the large bay window, then to his friend.

"Are we expecting company tonight? Did the Thatcher's say anything?"

"Not to me, they never. Besides, it is almost nine. Who would call at this time?"

"You never ordered a pizza, did you? I know what you are like," he teased.

Mark moved to the side of the window to look at who it may be. A large, dark saloon car had just pulled up outside the front entrance of the manor. A Mercedes.

"Well, whoever it is, they seem to drive a stylish car," he informed his host.

Callum joined him at the window, looking to see who it was at such a late time. He watched as two women stepped out of the car. From what he could make out, they seemed quite young —nobody he knew or expected. He threw his cue onto the table, sending it smashing into the balls left.

"Hey, I still had a chance of winning this game. So, let us call it a draw, then."

"Idiot. Come on, it must be important if two women rock up at this time of night."

Mark followed his friend out of the room and into the hallway of the house, not reaching the stairs before there was a knock on the door. Callum unlocked the doors and pulled the large oak door open to meet his visitors. It shocked him to see two young attractive nuns. They smiled at him, asking if he was Callum, not giving him time to answer. They strode past him into the hall.

"Yes, I am. Come in, won't you," he replied.

"I am sister Jade; this is my colleague, Sister Hannah. We are sisters from the Cistercian order of *Strictioris Observantiae*," Sister Jade said.

"Wow, trying to say that after four or seven beers," Marc added.

"You must be Marc, then," Sister Hannah added.

"So, what are two Benedictine sisters doing so far away from home?" Callum replied.

"As you appear to know of our order, then you will know we have had a long journey. We can disclose more over a cup of tea," Sister Jade replied.

Callum took them into the kitchen, where he did as the sister requested. They sat in silence for what seemed like ages. Neither Sister spoke; they just sat side by side at the table, drinking their tea. Marc looked across at Callum, who shrugged his shoulders. He put his finger to his lips, not wanting Marc to speak. He knew that when they were ready, they would reveal why they had called.

Callum was walking around the kitchen, putting things back in order, not wanting to anger Ms Thatcher when she came to make breakfast the next morning. Jade coughed, revealing she was ready to disclose her reason for the visit.

"We believe that there are people that are not as they seem, within the church. Something, or shall we say, somebody, is hiding their true intentions behind a veil of lies and deceit," Sister Jade said.

" OK, when you say 'we' believe, is that the royal 'we', as in the Vatican, or is this just a hunch?"

Sister Jade had a soft, friendly voice, and she seemed very approachable. She was attractive. Her facial features, even though masked by her coif and veil, were striking. She had perfect, blue eyes and high cheekbones. Her lips were full and tilted up, offering a permanent smile. Sister Hannah had a much sterner voice, one which you knew not to interrupt. It was she who replied:

"We do not act on hunches. We act on what we believe to be true," she replied.

"So, you are here to tell me what? That the church is corrupt? People have been saying that for a long time."

"No, Callum, nothing so petty. We know who you are, what you are and who your family is; long before you did, it seems. As you know who we are, too, I suspect."

Sister Jade rose from her chair, walked to the sink and washed her empty cup.

She continued, "The events that occurred here do not seem to be isolated to this area, Callum. Your cousins — your relatives — encountered the same situation."

"My relatives? There are more of these villages, more witches? Where?"

Sister Hannah laughed aloud, mocking the question. "You think you are the only one? Are you so naïve to think that you alone conduct this type of work? Now that you have cleansed your village, you are done, your work here is now finished," she said.

"Oh, I like her. She is funny," Marc said.

"No, not at all. I do not know what we expected. This is all new to me, so I would appreciate a little less hostility, if you please, sister."

Jade looked across at her compatriot, to silence her. She knew they needed Callum's help, as much as he would need theirs.

"Callum, we know it matters not who informs us. We know it to be true. That someone within our own fold is causing this occult manifesting. Be these witches or demons. Whatever evil they can summon, they are doing so."

"Sister Jade, what you are saying is that someone within the church is doing this. Why?"

"We have not figured this out yet. However, the level of evil that is spawning, or being called out of the darkness, shows it is one who has enough power and knowledge to be of great significance."

"And this relates to me how? I do not have that sort of knowledge, Sister."

"I think we are about to be inducted into something sinister, Callum," Marc added.

"Like the man said, what are we being asked to do?" Callum asked.

"Do you know of the priest, Liam Parsons?"

"The inquisitor. Yes, I have heard of his name, or read it somewhere in my uncle's books."

"You are to go to Dorset to the estate of the Young-Ballard family, on the Studland peninsula."

"I know where that is. It is not too far from here," Marc added.

"And do what? Find the priest and say what?"

Jade gave him an envelope with a red seal waxed at the fold at the rear. Three crowns flanked by two keys —the seal of the Vatican. He knew what it was. He asked the sisters just how important the journey was.

"When he has finished his current role, he needs to be given this letter. He will be with the lady of the manor. He is not to return to the Vatican," Sister Hannah informed him.

"No, at all costs, he is to travel with you to Pendle Manor, where you will meet up with the rest of your family," Sister Jade added.

230

"My family; I did not know there was a family," he replied.

"Well, of course there are others in the family. Distant relatives, but family none the less. And you all do the same job," Sister Hannah added.

"Yes, as Hannah said, there are others. Although they never came into this as late as you. But you need to get together and find where this evil is coming from."

"I take it that the priest does not know about this yet," Callum asked.

"No, he will go along with what we ask him to do," Sister Hannah said.

"You need to find out where this is coming from. Be that clerical, one of your kin or both, we must stop them, Callum."

"Do the family, as you call them, know I am coming?"

"Of course, otherwise what would be the point in sending you?"

Sister Hannah seemed angry at his questioning and was quick to show it. Callum responded in the same tone, explaining all this was new to him. It was as Sister Jade had said earlier. He had not come into this exceptionally long ago. And as this was his house, and they were guests, uninvited or not, she should change her attitude. He owed them no favours.

"We are a little on edge. I am sorry for Sister Hannah's tone. It is just the need to sort this out before they swamp us with dark forces. We are in the dark, ourselves, here. We need all the help we can get. You have proven your loyalty to us. We know you will do what needs to be done, Callum."

She handed him another envelope, explaining it contained all he needed to know about his distant relatives: backgrounds, names, and what they had been doing regarding their roles in the society.

Sister Jade dried her cup, placing it back on the shelf. She nodded across to Sister Hannah, showing it was time to leave.

"We will meet again at the manor in two days. That will give you time to collect Father Liam."

"So, we're leaving now — straight away?" Marc asked.

"Yes, you must. By the time you get to the coast, the priest would have finished his task at hand. He will not object," Sister Hannah replied.

"I am sure he will not. What else did he have planned, poor bloke?"

That was it. The sisters had said what they needed. They thanked them for the tea and the hospitality.

Callum and Marc watched as they drove away, still a little taken aback. The car made its way back down the driveway, the sound of the tires crunching on the gravel, breaking the silence of the night. The men walked back up the steps, closing the door behind them. They looked at each other in disbelief, then burst out laughing.

"What the fuck was all that about, then?" Marc asked.

"Well, it is good to know I have a family somewhere. I am confused what they think I, or we, can do about it all."

"We? What do you mean, we? I have nothing to do with all this weird crap."

"Ah, that was what you said weeks ago, and we know how that ended, mate, so pack a bag. We are leaving in an hour."

An hour later they were in Callum's car, driving towards the coast. Marc was asking him how a nun could look so sexy. He was convinced that he had a chance with Sister Jade.

"Did you see her, though? She was surprisingly good-looking for a nun. That outfit just seemed to cling to her body."

"Are you crazy, mate? You have no chance in hell. Well, hell, yes, but here, no chance. She is a resolute believer who has taken a vow of celibacy, Marc."

"Hey, you do not know that, do you? She may have had enough of all that and now wants out."

"All I can say is, keep your head in the game. We need to be focused here. If we are going to meet the rest of my clan, they may not be as friendly as we are. They seem to have been doing this for a long time."

"I know that. I am just saying that Jade woman was hot. For a nun."

"Yes, OK, she was. However, we are about to meet my family and powerful clergy types. If what those two penguins said is true, they are not what they seem. This will be a dangerous trip "I don't follow; what do you mean?" Marc asked.

"Think about it. That means they are as evil and dangerous as those bitches were in the pub. More so, as they are the ones in charge."

"Ah, yes. So what will happen if that is true? Will you have to take them out, or what?"

"I do not know, Marc; no idea. Everything is happening so fast. For both of us. But I can promise you one thing."

Callum pulled out onto the dual carriageway, putting the car into top gear, accelerating away into the night. He estimated they were less than two hours away.

"Marc, my friend, those guns in the boot will definitely be in use, and soon."

He was not sure what to expect, nor did he know how his relatives would greet him. It was a comfort knowing he did indeed have family, yet it was odd that they had never reached out to him before. Still, in time, he would know. The bigger issue here was what they expected him to do against a corrupt family member or church representative. Plus, did he have any right to do anything? There was a pecking order or something.

"Do not worry, mate. It will be fine. They will like you," Marc said.

Callum looked across at his friend slumped back in his seat beside him, drifting off to sleep. He smiled to himself, content that he had Marc with him. He may often speak before he thought about things, but he was a good friend. There was no way he would have got this far without him.

Marc sat up, let down his window slightly, then lit a cigarette. "You're welcome, mate. I would never let you do this alone."

Callum shook his head, smiled and lit his own smoke. The pair headed off in silence, each with their own thoughts.

CHAPTER 14

Steven backed away from the door, alarmed that this thing, or whatever it was, knew they were coming. He looked back at Justyna, who noticed his fear.

"Wait just a second. I need to be clear in my head on what is going to happen once we are in that room," he said.

"It is not just a demon, or is it? I am a little confused by that. Is a ghost a demon, and can they be the same? You said you saw ghosts here when you were young. Was it a demon back then, or just a ghost?"

Father Liam stepped back away from the door, putting his hand on Steven's shoulder. Calm as always, he explained:

"Spirits can be good or bad, like angels. Fallen angels are demons who serve Satan, or the devil, as you call him. So a ghost is not the actual dead spirit of a person. As Ecclesiastes 9:5-6 says, 'The dead know not anything, neither have they any more a reward; for the memory of them will be forgotten. Also, their love and their hatred and their envy, is now perished; neither have they any more a portion forever in anything that is done under the sun.'"

"Ghosts cannot harm you, so what about Martin and Edyta?" Steven asked the priest.

"Steven, the Bible teaches us that ghosts cannot be the actual dead person's spirit raised to life. They are the evil angels or demons pretending to be the dead who have come back to life in a spiritual form. These demons deceive people into believing that the soul lives on after death. This is Satan's and his evil demons' biggest lie — that when we die, our soul continues. We know this falsehood as the immortality of the soul."

"So, everything about ghosts is a lie, and the people who see them. What about that; even you? Plus, not all ghosts hurt people," Justyna added.

Father Liam sighed. It was confusing. Yes, he agreed with them that people saw ghosts. They existed, and yes, people saw them. He explained again that this was a demon's work, trying to attach itself to a human form

"The Apostle Paul tells us, that to be strong when Satan attacks, we must put on the full armour of God. Be strong in the Lord and in his mighty power. Put on the full armour of God, so that you can take your stand against the devil's schemes. For our struggle is not against flesh and blood, but against the rulers, against the authorities, against the powers of this shadowy world and against the spiritual forces of evil in the heavenly realms. Therefore, put on the full armour of God, so that when the day of evil comes, you may stand your ground, and after you have done everything, to stand. Stand firm then, with the belt of truth buckled around your waist, with the breastplate of righteousness in place, and with your feet fitted with the readiness that comes from the gospel of peace. Besides all this, accept the shield of faith with which you can extinguish all the flaming arrows of the evil one. Take the helmet of salvation and the sword of the Spirit, which is the word of God. And pray in the Spirit on all occasions with all kinds of prayers and requests. Be alert and always keep on praying for all the Lord's people."

"Wow, a lot to take in, but I get it. Believe in God, believe that this thing in there is a liar, and stand strong in our faith," Justyna replied.

"Yes, that is all you can do. You two must stand strong, together. Believe nothing you see or hear. He will attack you; I am sure. It is nothing more than a game to him. Leave the worry to me. Just put your faith in me." He blessed them. "In the name of the Father and the holy spirit, bless these children. Lord, keep them safe from harm. Amen."

They repeated the 'amen', and nodded that they were ready, yet Steven still thought it was not his fight. But he knew he had to help, somehow.

"Remember, terror is no joke. It is as real as we are. This is not a terrible movie or a creepy bedtime story. This is as real as anything you will ever know. I cannot say this enough — you must believe. Do you understand?"

They both nodded in agreement, but the priest wanted more than a nod of the head. He bellowed at them, catching them by surprise. This was the first time he had raised his voice. It scared them both.

"Do you understand? You must believe, always."

The priest opened the door, and they walked into the light. As they took their first steps into the room, the door slammed behind them. The guttural sound of a deep voice welcomed them. Steven and Justyna stood behind Father Liam who was scanning the room, looking for his foe. The room was hot — steaming hot — like a sauna. The light was coming from every direction, yet nowhere in particular. They backed around the room, huddled together, keeping close to the walls. Justyna mentioned there was no furniture in the room. It was bare. She was told by Father Liam to look up to the ceiling. On doing so, she saw that every piece of furniture was, what seemed to be, stuck to the ceiling. They backed into one corner of the room, where Father Liam felt he could see the entire room clear enough to challenge the demon. He stepped forward, calling for the demon to show itself.

"Come, Abaddon. Here I am — here we are. Your powers seem weaker now. Your hold over the trapped souls at The Chine is long gone. It is just you, now. Show yourself, banished angel."

Laughter met him. It seemed to come from every direction, as if the demon was surrounding them.

"When we last met, you may have taken a soul. Even that sin does not strengthen you more than I. It was me who was not ready. You were just a cheat and a liar who could only confront a novice. Come face me now, and let God forgive your fall from grace."

Again the room filled with laughter, although this time the light seemed to dim, as the centre of the room filled with a hazy wisp of black smoke. It twirled and entwined itself, thickening its size, until facing them was the face of Nathanial, his ghostly, dark appearance fading in and out of focus, as if floating through the light spectrum.

"You think I fell from grace?" He roared with laughter. He disappeared, only to reappear at the back of the room, then back into the middle of the room, facing them again.

"Why do you think they sent you to me so long ago, and now again? Because you were weak then, as you are now. That child's loss still sits with you, because you know I am stronger than your belief."

Father Liam stared at the apparition, trying to take in what the ghostly figure was telling him.

"Ah, you think it was just a coincidence that we met," the demon laughed.

"No, not at all. You are full of shit, and you will try to convince me that some corrupt hierarchy set me up."

"Do not mock me. I know how weary you have become. Wanting to go home to your sanctuary. I know everything. We know you and your misgivings."

Father Liam stepped forward, closer to the ghostly Nathanial. He held up his Bible, his beads wrapped around it, and a cross in the other hand.

"I have nothing to hide from you, hiding behind a tortured soul, weak as you are and always will be. For I am convinced that neither death nor life, neither angels nor demons, neither the present nor the future, nor any powers, neither height nor depth, nor anything else in all creation will separate us from the love of God that is in Christ Jesus our Lord," he shouted.

The demon Abaddon spoke for the first time, its voice perverted and garbled. The room smelt of sulphur, causing the trio to wretch.

"Your god does not love you. Why would you be here if this were true? No, he is fucking your mum — she begs for it," he laughed.

The voice was eerie — not a human voice. It seemed angry that someone dare question it.

"You are so boring, mortal. Even weak. You were always a weak, pathetic waster. Here you are, pretending to be a man of God. You dare challenge me. When I know the feelings you hide for the taste of the old woman's flesh. Tedious faker."

"Abaddon, they cast you out of heaven because you were weak. Your pitiful armoury is nothing, backed by a list of lies and deceit. In your own kind, you are just a second-class wanderer. Your powers do not challenge me."

"I have your friend here, girl. She wants to say hello. Even through her pain, she seeks you out," Abaddon answered.

"It is not her, Justyna. Just remember what he said," Steven whispered.

"Ah, the heir, the fresh blood. Slavers all. I wondered when you would dare enter our home. Creeping around the grounds. Spying, masturbating over your precious new slut."

The voice of Edyta filled the room, faint at first, gaining volume as she spoke through Nathanial and the demon.

"Why didn't you help me, Justyna? You left me, even when you needed me. I helped you."

"Ignore him. It is not your friend, Justyna," Father Liam interrupted.

"She likes it here with us. We love her. A thousand cocks will ravage her, filling her every desire. Friend, I think not."

The priest knew how strong this demon was. The archangel had cast him from heaven for wanting to kill the sinners on earth for their repetitive sinning. He was a trusted, beautiful angel who went against God, deciding to map his own form of justice, killing thousands of people.

"You know nothing of me, bastard. Do you think me so weak? You bring children to me. I see you hiding back there. Girl. Your friend is here. Come forward, join her. Drink with her."

Edyta's voice called out to Justyna, asking her to come find her. Her voice was erratic, panting in between sentences. Her voice was trembling, not with fear, but lust, excitement. The demon took over the conversation once more, taunting them.

"Your friend is fucking everyone, like you did before you came here. Drinking like a cheap slut, hoping that bastard beside you would come back and fuck you, make you the next grand lady of the estate. That old bitch at the house will not last long now, Steven. Then she will sit here. Her naked body sat on my thrusting erection. Your dear grandmother, taking it in her ass, like the priest wants to do to her."

The face of Nathanial was now gone, replaced by an ugly, armoured-covered face. The black armour seemed to grow out of the skin, rather than being an outfit. Only one eye was uncovered, and it was looking at Steven.

"Come on, boy, speak up. Do you want me to take the old bitch? It would make you rich. I can make you rich and give you everything you need — even that slut beside you."

"You have nothing I need. You are a sick fuck," Steven said.

Abaddon laughed once again. His giant wings flashed forward, whisking the stench of sulphur once more. A large chair dropped from the ceiling and flew toward all three of them. They all dropped to the floor in time, as the chair crashed into the wall behind them, covering them in the smashed debris.

"Why don't you let Nathanial go? He is no use to you now," Father Liam said.

"You order me. You know who I am, yet you still think you command me, Liam."

Once more the priest had outraged the demon, and his voice boomed his displeasure.

"God commands you; he commands you to release this man. I command you as Christ commands you. Leave this man; be gone from his captive soul. I command you in the Father's name. Christ, our God, demands you release this man."

Abaddon seemed to falter. His appearance changed back to Nathanial, then back to his own. Like a flickering TV channel, the image kept faltering. He screamed a list of profanities at the priest, his wings flapping behind him violently. Abaddon declared the man was a sinner, a murderer of children, and his soul belonged to Satan. There was no salvation for him.

Steven stepped beside the priest, declaring that his family had forgiven him, only for Abaddon to turn his attention to him. Steven went rigid, his body locked solid as he levitated off the floor. He rose into the air, his arms pulled out. As the demon turned him around and around, stretching Steven's arms beyond their natural limit, he screamed out in pain. He tried to speak; nothing came forward. And then he was sent flying backwards into the wall. He slumped to the floor as

Justyna screamed his name. The furniture above him from the ceiling came piling on top of him.

"You dare speak to me, you puny human. You are not devoid of sin. Reaping Granny's rewards, yet offering nothing in return."

Justyna rushed over to him, clearing away furniture, legs and broken glass.

"Ah, look at her, the wanting whore; Steven, Steven," Abaddon mocked.

"The family has no animosity toward you, Nathanial. You were wronged, and they are sorry. It has been too long now; leave this house. Regain your dignity, become the man again you were. Everything you gained will be as it was. Your legacy will continue," Father Liam shouted out.

Abaddon screwed his twisted face away from the Priest, screeching and screaming. "He is not leaving! He is mine! I own his tortured soul."

"His soul was never here, demon; it was never yours to take. In the name of Christ, our Father, I release him from you. My Lord, you are all powerful, you are God, you are the Father. We beg you, through the intercession and help of the archangels, Michael, Raphael and Gabriel, for the deliverance of our brothers and sisters who have been enslaved by the evil one. All saints of Heaven, come to our aid."

"You don't believe this. You're weak. Your prayers won't help you; he is mine."

Father Liam once again stepped closer to the demon. Again he thrust his Bible and cross towards Abaddon, flicking holy water across Abaddon's flesh. Abaddon screamed in a mixture of anger and agony.

"In the name of Jesus Christ, our God and Lord, Mary, our beloved mother of our Lord. Our blessed apostles and archangels and all saints. We command this demon to return to us the spirit of our son and leave this place of God. We drive you from us, whoever lay within you: unclean spirits, all satanic powers, all infernal invaders, all wicked legions, assemblies and sects."

"You know who I am. Your prayers are of no use here."

"God commands you, the Holy Trinity commands you, I command you: release to us the spirit of Nathanial Ballard." Father Liam continued throwing holy water at the demon. "By the misgivings of Nathanial, the mystery of incarnation, let all suffering of Nathanial be dissolved by Jesus Christ our Lord. I command you, demon, to release this man. Leave this house. We have no need of you, no need to fear you. We know your name, Abaddon; your powers are nothing to us. I know you as Abaddon. God commands you to release Nathanial."

Flames shot up and around the demon, so intense it blew the priest backwards. He tried to keep to his feet, yet the heat and stench were too much, and he crashed to the floor alongside Steven.

"Take him, you flea-ridden bag of bones. Keep him. He served his purpose. He brought me you."

The demon vanished, cursing and promising vengeance at the priest.

Liam helped Justyna get Steven to his feet. He asked him if he was OK, checking him over. Certain that he was fine, all three moved across the room to the garden side balcony doors.

"It pissed him off. Has he gone for help?" Steven asked, rubbing his arms and neck.

"No, he is here somewhere. He has just lost his vessel. Now it is just us and him."

The smell of sulphur returned, causing the trio to back away into the corner once more. All three looked around the room, anticipating the reappearance of the demon. They waited, all of them looking nervous, until the sound of something scurrying above them caused them all to look towards the ceiling. Above them, just three feet away from them, the twisted image of Abaddon looked down at them. His armoured head twisted around to face them. His torn black wings were stretched across the ceiling. His face dripped saliva onto the floor in front of them.

"Has the boy fucked you yet, Justyna? He wants to, you know. He dreams of raping you, daily. As does this fake inquisitor."

Abaddon voice hissed at them, garbled, as if three voices were repeating his words. Father Liam pushed the two away from the corner, following the wall to their left, trying to put space between them. The demon dropped to the floor, folding his wings behind him as it stretched upwards, showing his full form. His wings seemed matted yet full. His body was a mass of black scars which bulged across his ripped torso. It was plain to see he would have been a true angelic being if they had not cast him down from Heaven. He was tall and frightening to behold. Father Liam had to stand his ground. He knew he had to dismiss any thought of weakness now, not entertain any doubt in his mind, or consider why the demon was indeed here.

The demon stared them down, sauntering towards them. He looked angry. He did not think the three seemed worthy of his efforts to challenge him.

"You belong to me, faker. They promised your soul to me long before you thought you were a worthy adversary. I will take you and all your kind. Your own teachers cast you aside to my needs," he hissed. His voice was raised, spitting as he spoke, his black lips curled around black teeth as he continued to taunt the priest. "God does not want you. He has forsaken you, as much as your own kind at the Vatican has done."

As he spoke the words, various whispering voices laughed from within the demon's voice. They teased and repeated the demon's speech again. The demon, now enraged at the lack of response, shouted at the trio, mocking them all. Flames engulfed the demon's lower body; his wings fanned the flames towards them.

Father Liam stood his ground as he stood in front of Justyna and Steven. He looked over his shoulder, then smiled at the pair. "We believe, we have always believed." He cited the Lord's prayer.

Steven and Justyna both began taking over the prayer from the priest. Father Liam strode forward to the beast. Justyna began saying the prayer louder, hoping it may distract the demon from the priest. It failed. As it changed its attention to her, Justyna's body flew upwards, twisting around in the air. Her body slammed into the ceiling, her face smashing into the plaster, blood spewing from her face. She screamed out in agony as the demon dropped her to the floor. Steven tried to catch her before it caused her any further damage, only for them both to collapse in a heap.

Abaddon rasped at her; his voice was now venomous in anger. "Do not try me, child. You know nothing of me to dare cast pitiful prayers at me." He snapped his head back to face the priest, his unseen power ensnaring him, pulling him forward towards himself. "Enough now, godless one. You will now spend an eternity in pain. I will take time in your pain."

Father Liam smiled at the demon, confident in his own belief now. The demon had shown weakness in returning Nathanial to them. For once, he knew he had him.

"Abaddon, in the name of my God, the beloved virgin Mary, and Jesus Christ, I command you to leave this earth, in shame, and be gone to where the Lord cast you."

"I will never leave you, Liam, as you are mine — sworn to me," Abaddon hissed.

Father Liam blocked his opponent's voice from his mind, throwing the last of the holy water at him.

"I believe in my God, my church, along with my order. Your powers have no further hold here, demon. Under God's guidance and protection, your claims and lies mean nothing to me or these blessed children."

The demon roared, his body steaming from the holy water, his wings beating frantically. They made no difference, as he remained stationary, held to the spot. He cursed the church, he cursed the earth and every living sinner on it, demanding he be given what he was promised.

"Nothing you have been given is yours to have, demon, nothing. In the name of my Lord, be expelled now. Uprooted from this earth," the priest shouted.

Father Liam began walking forward. The demon tried to retreat, only to just contort himself, his wings now silent, the flames gone.

"Lord above, who cast this evil from your heaven, send him back to Satan, to the depths of hell."

Abaddon tried to protest, claiming he had been promised the souls of these sinners. He raised his voice, damning the priest and promising to return.

"We have no fear of you, Abaddon. We who know your name. Weak as you are, returning our beloved

Nathanial indeed proves your weakness, your lies and your deceit. Our faith is with God, our protector. It is he who sends you back, through me. I send you back. The virgin Mary sends you back."

"Sinner, it is not over! I will be back — we will be back!" Abaddon roared.

"Retire now, surrender in the name of the Father. Be gone forever. Your time here is over," the priest shouted, over the pleading voice of the demon.

The room exploded into a haze of smoke and bright light. The sound of a mass of voices, crying and screaming, deafened them. Each voice was denying the fact that the priest had beaten Abaddon, crying his name in pity and shame. Then, nothing.

Father Liam sank to his knees, exhausted in his triumph. Justyna and Steven slowly crawled across to him, nervously looking around the room.

"Has he gone? Was that it? Will he be back?" Steven asked.

"Son, for crying out loud, what more do you want? Was that not enough for one day?"

Justyna pushed Steven, shooting him a look to shut him up. She got to her feet, offering her hand to the priest. He took her hand, pulling himself upright. He looked older, drained and tired.

"We should go, Father, there is nothing here to stay for now."

"Yes, we all need to go; at least get a little fresh air. The stench of that demon still lingers."

Steven whispered to Justyna, asking if that meant the demon was still here. She just shook her head in disbelief, not even answering. She pushed him towards the door. They made their way to the downstairs corridor. Justyna stopped at the top of the stairs. Her bottle of spiced rum was still on the top stair.

"You are the only thing I am taking from here, my friend," she said.

As they made their way to the reception foyer, she pulled Steven back. "Wait, look. Somebody is waiting for you."

She pointed over to the lounge, where the ghostly figure of Wyn was stood. She waved across to them, a last farewell. As Steven waved back, Wyn was joined by Nathanial. He stood dressed in all naval regalia. He never waved. He just lowered his head, before both images faded away.

"He has nothing to say? Not a sorry, or whatever?" Steven asked

"It is better that way. He was just a tool — a ghost who was not permitted to move on. His punishment is to remain here. Nothing he can say will give him peace. He knows this."

" OK, but what about his friend? The voodoo gods took him," Justyna said.

"Well, not gods. Come on, after all that we just went through. There is but one God. Yes, he was taken. I suspect it was due to him doing something that he could have said no to, where Nathanial was possessed. So, it was seen as a choice for him."

"Are we forgetting about Martin? Where is he?" Steven asked.

"Yes, indeed. Something is wrong there; I am not sure what, though. However, I think we will find out later."

"Sorry, I do not quite follow you. Is he dead or just gone somewhere?" Steven asked.

"For now, my son, I suggest you forget about Martin. Concentrate on what you have here. Build a new empire as your gran asks from you. This chapter is finished," Father Liam told him.

They were outside. The chilly air was refreshing; cold but refreshing. The snow had stopped, and the white blanket that covered the grounds was picturesque.

All three made their way across the gardens to the woods, to take the path to the manor. They discussed the events, asking if they were ever more scared. The priest said they should be scared, but if they believed, they would always succeed against evil.

As they reached the path, Steven pointed out a set of footprints which lead from the back of the hotel, across the garden lawns, and into a woodland track further along the fence.

"Martin — it must be," Justyna said.

"Time will tell. His path is one not of our doing. He is on a dark journey."

"Do we go after him, or what?" Steven asked.

"No, we will find out at the proper time where his loyalties lay. Forget him. You will not see him again."

The walk back was a silent one for the priest, time to reflect on the demon's words. He listened to the other two joke and laugh, Steven now a brave hero in his own head, while Justyna mocked him. They were going to be fine; he was sure of this. A good couple with a great future. For the priest, it was more of a concern to know that someone in the church had contact with such a high-ranking demon. Someone who promised the demon his soul. How was this possible in the church today? Or possible in any day. Did this mean the church was corrupt? Were priests dealing in black magic? He was tired and drained — nothing was making sense. He knew that when he returned to Rome, he would find the answers.

They reached the manor house, where Beryl had seen them coming. She was on the steps waiting for them, relieved they were all safe and back home.

Beryl kissed and hugged Justyna, then the others in turn. She ushered them all inside. Drinks were offered before she asked for a complete report on what had happened.

"Please, Gran, can we all freshen up, have a drink and shower first?"

"We will tell you all about it, we promise," Justyna replied.

"I think a small sleep would be a welcome gesture, Beryl," Father Liam said.

"Of course, I am so sorry. I just am so happy you all got back safe. When you're rested, over dinner then."

They all thanked her and made their way to the rooms upstairs to rest and freshen up. The priest was the last to make his way upstairs, letting the youngsters go ahead while he at relaxed by the fire. He finished his drink, then left the room to follow suit. As he passed the dining room, he noticed, through the open double doors, that the table has been set for seven people. He knew it — something was wrong about the whole situation. He continued to his room, pausing to listen at the door of one of the spare rooms. After hearing the whispered voices from within, he knew it was not over yet. He hoped there was a bottle in his room. He needed another drink — a strong one.

He opened his door, walked to his bed and just collapsed across the mattress. Tired, he rubbed his eyes, the smell of Sulphur still with him. After stretching his arms above his head, he clicked his neck bones, as he twisted his head from side to side. What more did they want from him, these mysterious guests? Not ready for sleep just yet, he rolled to his side, propping himself up on his elbow. Yes, it was there — the bottle of whisky. Good, old Beryl, she knew him so well.

It was still early in the day. So, two or three drinks, sleep, shower, then dress for dinner. He also knew there would be a clean suit and collar in the wardrobe. Beryl would have seen to that, too. Only then would he find out what the strangers were doing here. It was hard not

255

to think about it. But if they were here and nobody was talking about it, then it was dark.

CHAPTER 15

Father Liam was the last to attend the dining room. He entered, went straight to the cocktail bar then poured himself a stiff, large drink. Downing it in one, he poured a repeat then took his seat at the table.

"So early, Father. Is it wise to drink so heavily, or at all, for a man in your position?" Sister Hannah asked.

"So, what are we having to eat? I really am quite famished, Beryl," he asked.

"Your favourite, Liam — Beef wellington," she replied.

"Ah, perfect. How are you two feeling? It was a particularly challenging time. I must say, you were both extraordinarily strong."

"I am glad we had your help, Father. It was terrifying, to be honest."

Sister Hannah flushed red at being ignored in such a way; a fact not missed on by the rest of the room. She was about to ask again, only for Sister Jade to place her hand on her shoulder, shaking her head slightly to silence her. Sister Hannah screwed her lips up in anger at the rebuke. Yet she remained silent.

The meal was served. The priest, along with Steven and Justyna, informed the table of the events that they had faced earlier. Question after question was fired at them, all which they were happy to answer. It was when they were finally done with the questioning that the sisters held court.

"The demon told you that he was promised your soul, yet he failed to inform you from who?" Sister Jade enquired.

"It would seem so," he answered.

"Have you any belief that what he said was true?" Sister Hannah asked him.

"A demon rarely speaks the truth, if at all. Yet, I see you think otherwise, Sister."

"We have information that may yet prove otherwise, yes," Sister Jade replied.

"Can I ask why two sisters of your sect are here at all? This is not the work that I am led to believe you are currently tasked with."

"Our work is as the Lord directs. We have many roles to play," Sister Hannah said.

"I am well aware of what your work is, and I have no doubt that it has nothing to do with the haunting of The Chine."

"You are well known to us, Father Liam, as we are to you. We need to talk alone. This matter is of no interest to these kind people," Sister Hannah said.

"And so, ends this dinner," he replied.

"Has this man not done enough for you people? It is time he was left in peace," Beryl shouted.

She stood and walked around the table to stand beside her old friend. It was clear to the sisters that they were old friends — a point that sister Hannah made note of, concerned that the relationship was more than it should be.

Father Liam calmed his friend, then suggested that they retire to the library to speak privately. Beryl was told that he was fine with it. The church always came first, she knew that. Still, she made a point of showing the sisters that she was unhappy.

Steven and Justyna took her into the lounge where they said they wanted to talk to her, in the hope that she may relax and take her mind off what the sisters had in store for her friend.

Father Liam sat across from the sisters. He guessed they were here for a far more sinister reason than the events that had just happened in The Chine. He looked at Sister Jade. He could see she was far more than just a nun serving an order. She looked younger than her age, her beauty hidden by her attire. For a nun of her kind, she was obviously well-informed and aware of the work that involved the occult. Her colleague was sterner, one who obviously followed every word of her order.

"You asked me about my soul belonging to the demon, Abaddon. Why do you see this as a concern, or even a truth?"

"Did he bring the subject up constantly? Did he refer back to any time or date?" Sister Jade asked.

"Look, it was a demon in all his form. He said things. I do not write or record what they say, Sister."

"Yes, I know that. Let me put it this way. Is it normal for an inquisitor to encounter a demon for a second time? One who is happy to give its name so freely?"

"You know the answer to that," he said.

"Our point exactly, Father. He wanted to tell you. He had a motive. Demons do not work in this way, as you know. He was sent to you."

"I knew something was wrong, but sent to me? You think Satan is sending demons to seek me out?"

"Not Satan, Father, no. One of our own," Sister Jade told him.

"That is absurd! Who can do that? From where can they do that?" he shouted.

He went to the decanter, pouring himself a drink; again, downing it in one gulp, before pouring another.

"My drinking is my business, Sister, before you pass judgement. When you have done the work I do, or even try to face Satan's finest, then you may comment. Until then, please refrain from making a judgement."

"Father, we do not come here to offend you. Sister Hannah just wants to be sure we have your full attention."

"Go on. You were saying that someone is sending demons to hunt me down."

"Not quite, but we do believe that someone, or a sect or group —we are not sure —are causing a range of dark forces to rise."

"What sect? Where is this happening? This is news to me."

"We believe it is coming directly from the church, Father, the Vatican's higher echelon," Sister Hannah added.

"Nonsense, not possible."

"As Reverend Gabriel Amorth said long ago: the devil resides in the Vatican, Father."

Sister Jade went on to explain the issue of Cardinals who did not believe in Jesus and bishops linked with devil. It was said that as far back as 1972, Pope Paul VI talked about the 'smoke of Satan'. Sister Hannah explained the evil of the paedophile scandals and Swiss guards accused of murder, and so much more; that evil was rife.

"The fact that the devil has indeed penetrated the Vatican halls, is making the most reverent priest look for answers and the truth."

"Good grief, are you sure of this? Do you know of any such priests who have turned their backs on God?"

"This is the sad part, Father, we do," Sister Jade said.

"This is why we are here. We need your help."

"Of course. I was never going home, was I?"

"I know not of what you may have been promised, Father."

"So, what is it you want from me, Sisters?."

"Do you know of the Hopkins legacy?" Sister Jade asked him.

"Indeed. the Hopkins witch finders — hunters. Call them what you will."

"Across the country, they have various estates and lands, from one end of the country to the next. Each estate has had a revival, a resurgence, or a regeneration of covens; one seen as a rare thing. A local black witch is dealing with something they think is fun, unaware of the true dangers," Sister Hannah informed him.

"The newest member of the Hopkins family is on his way here to meet you. You are to travel to Pendle Manor, in the middle of Dartmoor."

"What? Me? Why? What do you think I can do? This is not my field," he explained.

"Father, it is. The whole Hopkins family will also be in attendance, summoned by the family elder, to find the underlying cause of this. Plus, if the church seniors are involved, it is for sure that a demon possesses them already."

"That is a big ask. Are you sure I am the right priest to help you here?"

ˈ "Monsignor Cavalli has assured us you are the one who must do this. He feels you are the only one he trusts, to be honest — to do what is required," Sister Jade said.

She passed him an envelope. Again the seal of the Vatican was on the fold at the back.

"All you need to know is in this. The Hopkins boy will soon be here. You can discuss the letter with him on your journey."

"So that is it, then. I am going, even if I do not want to."

"The Monsignor did say you would function as you are. He said to offer his regret. But this must be done, Father."

"What is your role in all of this? You never came all this way just to inform me of the next job for me. You have a part to play in this, I take it."

Sister Jade began to tell him the initial plan. They were going ahead to Pendle Manor, where they would function as housemaids. They would blend in and find out as much information as possible, from behind the scenes. They were not to talk to each other openly. Every ounce of secrecy was to be maintained. They were to trust nobody, other than themselves. Only Callum Hopkins and his aide, Marc, were aware of the involvement of the sisters. Kevin Hopkins, the family elder, was aware, obviously. He was the one who had become aware of the instability in the family. He had approached the Monsignor with his concerns. It was then that the Monsignor and his bishops agreed that dark forces were indeed at work. It was something that only a knowledge of the secrets hidden in the church's vaults would hold. Only a select few had that sort of access. Someone was not who they appeared to be, which was a suspicion long held by the Monsignor. As the Hopkins and the church were linked by the secrets of a lifetime, it was time to hatch a plan to flush the evil out. The Hopkins family had been doing the church's work for generations, protected by the higher order of the Vatican.

So as the family had a new member, it was custom for the family to meet, offer advice, help — if needed — and introduce themselves to their kin. It was a perfect time to seek the dark forces that were behind this resurgence.

Father Liam said he still found it hard to accept that the church was behind the problem, though he would do as was requested. What choice did he really have? After The Chine, he knew his faith was strong.

The sisters left. They had nothing further to say or add. They would see him again later at the Manor, set in the middle of the moors. It was secluded and private.

Father Liam went to find Beryl, explaining he had to go. He had been summoned back to the Vatican, as he thought. They wanted to know about The Chine, in case something else like it happened. He hated lying to his oldest friend, yet he now had to only trust those who knew the task ahead.

It was an hour before Callum turned up at the house. Father Liam had already made his farewell speeches to all inside the house. He blessed them all, promising to see them again soon.

He was stood in the driveway as Callum pulled alongside him. The window wound down, and the smiling face of Callum Hopkins stared out at him.

"You must be Father Parsons, I presume."

"Indeed, I am, young man. Nice to meet you."

With the introduction done — be it brief — he opened the back door to climb in. Marc jumped out, ran around to the priest, took his case and placed it in the boot. Marc waved to the people on the steps before he jumped back in the vehicle. Then they drove off, back down the long driveway.

"How are you doing, Father? I am Marc, Callum's right-hand man. You've been busy."

"Yes, son, you could say that."